The Return of Lieutenant Boruvka

JOSEF SKVORECKY

The Return of Lieutenant Boruvka

Translated and adapted
by Paul Wilson

faber and faber
LONDON · BOSTON

This English translation First published
in Canada in 1990
by Lester & Orpen Dennys Limited, Toronto
First published in England in 1990
by Faber and Faber Limited
3 Queen Square London WC1N 3AU
Originally published in Canada in 1981
as *Navrat porucika Boruvky*
by Toronto: 68 Publishers

Photoset by T. H. Best Company Limited, Canada
Printed in England by Clays Ltd, St Ives plc

A CIP record for this book is available from the
British Library

ISBN 0-571-14974-X

Contents

1

Kid Sister

My kid sister was found by Mrs. Rose Etherington, who goes to Jirina McCavish's house in Cabbagetown every Tuesday morning to restore something resembling order to the place. Heather was sprawled on the kitchen floor just beside the table, where she had apparently collapsed. The cleaning lady was unperturbed; she'd found her like that before. First she read the note stuck conspicuously to the hall mirror with chewing gum. "Mrs. Etherington," it said, "Had to go to Kitchener, not back till tomorrow, money in usual place, J."

Then she went in to deal with Heather.

It was only when she touched her that she felt alarmed. And when she turned her over, she saw the blood.

My kid sister had died in a way that was more or less consistent with the way she'd lived.

Harrison Morrison and I had been talking about Heather that very morning, at the Iroquois Racquet Club. Harrison had admired her ever since she used to play field hockey for St. Hilda's. That seemed like centuries ago, but his affection had persisted— probably because he'd never got any further than staring at her

1

knees during the hockey matches. He had followed her career with the tenacity of a faithful bulldog, and—spurred by what had once been jealousy but was now merely a fetish—he'd become a walking list of all the men who, while not necessarily admiring my kid sister, had climbed to far greater heights with her. According to him, there'd been enough of them to make up at least two complete rugby teams.

Still, all these blows to his heart hadn't managed to turn him into a young Werther—who, if I remember correctly from my European Lit survey course (unfortunately I dropped it six weeks into the first semester), entered a monastery because of some young woman not unlike Heather. Harrison consoled himself by marrying into a thirty-five per cent interest in the Limbo Springs Brewery, and by turning his love for Heather into a hobby and wasting his time keeping track of her affairs—not to mention annoying me with the details.

We were unwinding under the showers after our game when Harrison began, in that sleazy, indirect way he has. "I have to admit I don't know who number twenty-nine is. He's not from Toronto, as far as I can tell, and he certainly doesn't look like one of us."

"Oh, for Christ's sake, Harrison," I snapped, "why don't you try collecting something else for a change? Fossils or first editions of pornography—anything." His prurient interest was beginning to get on my nerves. Besides, I had problems of my own. Sheila—my girlfriend—had told me she was having second thoughts, as they say, about our relationship. "I'm sorry, Neil," was how she'd put it, "but I'm going through so many changes and it's just not fair to you." Straight out of a feminist rag on how to dump your man without bruising his ego, right? It was an improvement on the old days, though, when she used to blame everything on five thousand years of male supremacy. Anyway, I told her to relax and invited her to spend a couple of weeks with me in Mexico. So she was leaving Sue in charge of the agency and coming along. But the truth of it was that I was having second thoughts about Mexico and all its distractions. Perhaps we should be going on a wilderness trek instead.

Harrison ignored my remark. "Southern European type, I'd say. Intense, with passionate black eyes and a foreign accent. He sounded Slavic, I thought."

I had to laugh. When it comes to foreign languages, Harrison is as deaf as a post. The closest he's ever come to anything Slavic was an undergrad course in Russian he once took. He told me he'd lasted about four weeks.

"Classic lady-killer, Gable with an accent," he went on. "But he's got one flaw: somebody must have stepped on his nose. It hasn't got a bridge at all—more like an underpass."

"Harrison Morrison," I said—I know he hates the rhyme in his name; his father, an amateur linguist who revelled in puns and palindromes, gave it to him as a joke—"why don't you change stations? You're boring me. And besides, it's none of your business, and none of mine either. Frankly, I don't give a damn what she does, or whom she does it with."

That was a lie. The fact was that I was almost too fond of Heather. Once she had been a sweet little girl who believed in romance, and I'd kept my fingers crossed for her as she blundered through all her puppy loves. Then she began to adjust to the real world and I lost track of her comings and goings, but they troubled me. If anything, they bothered me more than they did my father. I had even shouted at her on occasion, which is more than he could ever bring himself to do. When he suffered, he suffered in silence.

"I wonder where he's from," Harrison persisted. "I got a close look at him last night in the lounge at the Four Seasons, and I tell you, this guy must have a line of trophies at home a mile long, know what I mean? I'll bet even Heather goes weak in the knees when he turns those mafioso eyes on her, and she's been around. Too bad about his nose...."

I was just about to rearrange Harrison's own nose when they began paging me over the loudspeakers. "Would Mr. Neil Donby please come to the manager's office for an important phone call." Harrison's face was saved.

I quickly finished dressing and walked to the office. No wonder my otherwise accommodating kid sister had categorically excluded that fool Harrison from her affections.

In the manager's office I learned what had happened. It felt as if a piece of my own life had just been ripped away.

Harrison Morrison was also the first to offer the opinion that what I did as soon as I came to my senses was reckless and stupid. He may have been right. Perhaps I should have left the whole thing to the police. But at the time it seemed like the natural thing to do. I called Sheila, and when she had fought back the tears, she told me that of course we must cancel our vacation. She also offered to do anything she could to track down the murderer. Perhaps I should have tried to dissuade her, but in my grief—which was deeper than anyone, least of all Morrison, could imagine—I was so grateful for her support and understanding that I didn't stop to think whether it was the proper thing to do.

I should explain that Sheila runs a female detective agency, called "The Watchful Sisters". The sinister name isn't my fault; I tried to persuade her to call it something else, but to no avail. Sheila, for all the years have mellowed her, is still too much of a radical feminist to welcome advice from males.

The Watchful Sisters is the first female detective agency in Toronto—maybe in the world, for all I know. I had my misgivings when she started it, but basically I was glad she'd gone into business. The agency represented an advanced stage of her natural evolution away from the bloodthirsty ideals she had espoused in the early seventies, beginning with the Weathermen (whom she could only admire from a distance anyway) and winding on through the League of Young Socialists, the Union of

Friends of Hoxha's Albania, and a number of other like-minded clubs, all of them founded on the principle that mathematical political certainties exist. That was her stormy youth. Now, approaching early middle age (she's twenty-seven), she's just a feminist with the usual vaguely leftist political views. Her most recent excursion into female bonding is a sorority called the Socialist Women's International Federation of Trade, or SWIFT—a club of women around their early thirties who are anxious to get on with their careers without appearing to abandon their ideals. It's supposed to be a strictly political set-up, but whatever it is, the members seem more interested in networking than in revolution. So it was a natural step from there to the private capitalist firm of the Watchful Sisters. A substantial inheritance from her parents made that step easier.

Gradually, as the rough edges of Sheila's idealism have been worn smooth, it's become possible to hold a conversation with her once more. She's begun to sense, I think, that apart from my business acumen, acquired over a number of years with a prestigious Bay Street brokerage firm, I have other qualities to offer as well, qualities that her soul-mates in SWIFT can't match. My persistence is beginning to pay off, and I have definite hopes that Sheila may reward my efforts by joining me in that most bourgeois of institutions, holy matrimony.

All of Sheila's shamusesses are University of Toronto graduates in criminal psychology, and they're all members of SWIFT. Even Sue, the ethnic secretary, is a member, though I suspect she had rather base and dishonourable motives for joining the group: she needed the job.

There's only one flaw in the sexual purity of Sheila's agency: she has a secret agent in the Toronto Homicide Squad. His name is Bill Kendrick—Sergeant Bill Kendrick—and his masculinity is beyond suspicion. From time to time—quite often, in fact—he slips the Sisters minor leads. Of course, the information always comes from other departments, since no one has ever hired

Sheila on a murder case. Until now, that is. Like all private investigators, Sheila's girls usually handle things like insurance fraud, missing persons, and the occasional adultery—although for ideological reasons they work only for suspicious wives, never for suspicious husbands. Her most conspicuous success has been the smashing of a child-porn ring based in the sleepy suburb of Willowdale. Again, it was Kendrick who gave her the keys to that case—which might be considered a breach of professional ethics on his part, but he's never accepted payment for his help, and does it only because he's sweet on Sheila, who in turn rewards him with just enough hope to keep him interested and to keep the information flowing. Some people might think I have cause for jealousy, but frankly, I've never lost any sleep over Bill Kendrick.

So I think it was logical to accept Sheila's help. In that first surge of grief and rage, I had to do something. Hiring Sheila meant I could have a direct hand in helping her; and besides, I love Sheila and I want to see her do well. Why should the police—whose record in solving murders leaves a lot to be desired—get all the glory?

Yet I did wonder briefly if Sheila was temperamentally suited to the job of tracking down a cold-blooded murderer. She still believed—despite her militant war against male violence—that all murderers were victims of their environment, be it poor, rich, or middle-class.

At first, it looked as though Sheila's part in the case would be short-lived. Within hours the Homicide Squad had come up with a prime suspect, as Sheila discovered when she phoned Bill Kendrick to tell him that she'd taken on the case.

I knew the suspect. Amid the tangle of my kid sister's male acquaintances, the fiftyish Herman Chumac was about as incon-spicuous as Charles Manson at a Sunday-school picnic. It wasn't his age that made him stand out, for (as Harrison Morrison was always reminding me) my twenty-one-year-old sister had at least one over-ripe septuagenarian among her suitors. But during one of the violent arguments that used to characterize all Heather's relationships, Chumac had actually beaten her up, leaving her slightly deaf in one ear. At the time Sheila had urged her to press charges, and for once I agreed with her, but Heather refused.

Despite the brutality, they apparently made up; not long before my kid sister was murdered, I saw them both in a lovey-dovey mood in the revolving restaurant at the top of the CN Tower, where Sheila had invited me to help her entertain an out-of-town client. My eyes still mist up when I think about it.

They were sitting there by the huge glass panels with Toronto slowly revolving beneath them: Heather, my pretty, blonde, petite little sister, and a nondescript, rather beefy fellow with a nose like a slab of jellied meat. The only hair he had left was a set of greying sideburns. The two of them were billing and cooing—there's no other way to describe it—like a pair of pigeons. They were laughing and kissing over their glasses of wine when Chumac pulled a lady's handbag from somewhere under the table and Heather began rummaging through it nosily. She pulled out some photographs and they both looked at them, giggling and carrying on while the lovesick Bluebeard placed fresh kisses on her wrists. Then he got up, looked around, and walked off with the handbag.

Everything about this little scene enraged me. It wasn't just that they appeared to be poking about in other people's private things; the truth was that I couldn't stand to see my sister carrying on in public with this old thug as though she were a high-class whore. As soon as Herman disappeared with the purse, I got up and walked over.

I still get chills when I recall our conversation. "Aren't you ashamed of yourself, kid?" I said.

She was wearing wide, dark glasses to hide the bruises and she obviously hadn't noticed me until then. At first she was startled, then her face darkened. "What are you doing here, Neil, spying on me?"

"Just admiring your taste, Heather. Look, for Christ's sake, the guy's a brute. Stay away from him."

"Get off my back, Neil." She turned away and looked out the window. Beneath us in the summer dusk, the black office towers revolved slowly, like enormous coffins.

"What's next, Sis? Your nose? An eye? Or maybe just a few teeth?"

Heather turned back to me abruptly and snapped, "Next time he'll kill me. But that's my own fucking business. You mind yours."

At the time, the fury of her reply shocked me. I hardly even listened to the words.

The police picked up Chumac an hour after they arrived at the scene of the crime; a neighbour had seen him walking out of Jirina's garden late in the evening. So the case appeared to be over almost before it had begun. Chumac didn't deny being there, but insisted that he hadn't killed my sister. His story was that she had called him up earlier in the evening and told him she had just left home, a rather common occurrence in Heather's case, and was going to sleep at Jirina's house on Sackville Street. But Jirina had gone to Kitchener and Heather said she didn't feel like spending the night alone. Chumac promised to keep her company, but there was a banquet in progress at the Old English Pub where he was manager and he couldn't get there until after ten that evening.

When he arrived, the house was dark. He knocked on the front door, which had a door-knocker instead of a bell. No one came, so he walked around to the back. It was the last in a row of tiny old refurbished townhouses crowded up against a crumbling wall surrounding St. James's Cemetery, and its south side faced a narrow laneway leading to the garages in the back.

He slid open the latch on the backyard gate, walked up to the french doors leading to the kitchen, and tried to open them. They were locked, and a curtain was drawn across them on the inside. Herman tapped on the glass, but the only sign of life was Jirina's brindled tomcat, who slipped through the curtains, put its pink paws against the glass, and gave a shrill miaow. The moon was full and the animal wanted out. Its wail mingled with the quiet humming of an air conditioner in an upstairs bedroom window. Herman tried the doors again, with no luck. He knew my sister well enough, he said, to conclude that she was no longer in the mood for a night of love and had instead turned to other sources of pleasure, probably of a pharmacological nature. He tapped once more while the white-faced cat regarded him motionlessly through the smudged glass. Then he decided that further knocking was pointless and left the backyard the way he had come. Just as he was closing the gate, a neighbour looked out the window of the house on the other side of the lane. He knew her by sight and waved, then walked back to his car, which was parked on Sackville Street. He drove back to the restaurant in time to hear the end of a debate among several of his regular patrons on whether it had been wise to dismantle the Austro-Hungarian Empire after the First World War. This last detail of his story seems far-fetched only until you know that, like Herman, most of the customers at the Old English Pub are Czechs.

On the other side of those french doors, beyond the curtain, lay my kid sister, with a .45 slug in her heart. Her killer had shot her at point-blank range, leaving powder burns on her blouse. It looked to me like a situation straight out of the detective classics: the front door was bolted, the french doors were secured by a safety catch on the inside, and none of the windows had been jimmied. But the police didn't look at it that way. They simply concluded that the murderer must have had a key.

Chumac denied owning a key, but he couldn't very well deny being there, since the neighbour had spotted him. On the other hand, the police didn't have the murder weapon and they couldn't prove Chumac had ever owned a pistol, so they reluctantly released him with a warning not to leave Toronto. Sheila was back in business.

Sheila asked me what I knew about Herman Chumac. As a matter of fact, I knew quite a bit. When he tried so persistently to reinstate himself in my kid sister's favour, I made it my business to make enquiries.

"Ever since he took over as manager of the Old English Pub it's been English in name only," I told Sheila. "It's the headquarters for the Czech mafia in Toronto. That's what Jirina McCavish says."

Sheila looked at me suspiciously and said, "How come you know this McCavish woman, anyway?" The question pleased me. The Thoughts of Chairperson Germaine were obviously far from her mind these days.

"Jirina's late husband was a schoolmate of mine, Tim McCavish. He raced planes and had the reputation of being something of a dare-devil. Unfortunately he was also accident-prone. When he was still at St. Patrick's, he broke his leg at a school dance. He made a fortune in aircraft design, most of it in the U.S.A. And he met Jirina at Expo '67; she was working in the Czechoslovakian pavilion. She was his next accident. Her attitude to marriage," I added, "is a lot different from yours."

Sheila looked at me with her cool blue eyes and replied icily, "Okay, tell me about this 'mafia'. That could be important."

"I doubt it. It sounds more like a mutual aid society to me. Most of the staff at the Old English Pub, from the bar-girls to the chef, are Czechs, and so are most of the regulars. It seems they're used to hanging out in bars and cafés back home, and when they get to Toronto they go out and spend most of their time among their own kind. According to Jirina, they're always doing each other favours. I guess that's why she calls it the Czech mafia; it doesn't seem to have much to do with outright crime. Like the chef, for instance."

"What about him?"

"Herman apparently saved him from suicide in New York."

I had heard the chef's story from Jirina, who's a bottomless pit of gossip and anecdotes. It seems she runs them in her newspaper, which she started up with money earned from a few of Tim's patents and other securities she inherited after his crash. You might say she inherited me as well, since I've continued to handle her portfolio for her. I might add that I've done rather a good job of it.

Jirina is certainly one of the strangest clients I've ever had. She makes absolutely no distinction between her business and personal life, so I often feel more like a friend than a financial adviser. I find myself arguing with her in a way I would never do with anyone else. I used to think I had some pretty sensible opinions on how the world worked, yet sometimes when I ask her a perfectly straightforward question she treats me like an innocent child—or, even worse, a halfwit, a hopeless tenderfoot who needs to be led by the hand through the pitfalls of world politics.

So I've learned to limit my advice to financial matters, where I'm sure of myself. As for her newspaper, it's beyond me. It has a strange name—*Torontska Dama*—which means something like *Toronto Lady*. I gather it could stand proud beside our own worst scandal sheets. She even has subscribers in South Africa, where she claims the Czechs are one of the strongest immigrant groups. When Sheila heard this, she remarked how typically Czech it was to choose a new homeland like that, given how right-wing they all were. You'll have to forgive Sheila; most of the Czechs she's met make McCarthy look like a pink liberal.

Naturally I can't read *Toronto Lady*, so everything I know about the editor's canards is from her own accounts. She, of course, swears they're all truer than the truth. That's nonsense; how can anything be truer than the truth?

Anyway, on this particular day I had come specifically to ask Jirina about Herman Chumac. He was beginning to worry me, and with her connections in the Czech community, I thought she might know something about him. She gave me a rather odd look and said she did, but before she could tell me anything essential she got sidetracked into a long, rambling tale that she seemed to think explained everything, whereas it just left me more confused than ever. It had something to do with tearing down some official state theatre in Prague. The wreckers had unearthed a luxurious sauna that had been built secretly for members of the Central Committee so they'd have somewhere to get cosy with the ballerinas. Jirina claimed the story was highly believable because she had it straight from her best inside source, also a member of the Central Committee, though of course he'd never used the sauna himself.

"Still being faithful to you, eh?" I asked. I love to banter with her.

Jirina tapped her forehead impatiently, and when I asked her, rather testily, what she meant by that, she said, "Do you think an ex-lover would send me news of a political scandal, knowing I would rush it into print? They know who all my ex-lovers are; I was very thoroughly screened before they cleared me to work at Expo '67. If I'd had a lover in the Central Committee, they'd—"

"Who are 'they'?" I interrupted.

"The secret police, of course!" said Jirina, somewhat annoyed. "If my source inside the Central Committee had ever been my lover, they would have put two and two together and *phhht!*" she snapped her fingers, "goodbye inside source. No, he's not my lover, he's—" and she stopped, turned pale, and said, "Oh Christ, there I go shooting off my mouth again." And she made me give my word of honour not to say a word about her informant.

"A private sauna is nothing unusual in itself," she went on. "The members of the Central Committee and their friends have a private hospital, private dentists, a private hotel, and special passes to diplomatic shops that sell fine goods and booze, so one more private sauna is peanuts. Who cares? As a matter of fact, the average Joe probably feels more envy than outrage. Can you imagine being thrashed with birch boughs by a bevy of nubile national artists? But when they tore the sauna apart, they found one of those same national artists under the floor. She'd been missing for some time and it was thought she'd betrayed her country."

"Betrayed her country how?"

"Oh, in their lingo it just means they thought she'd emigrated to the West without asking the authorities for permission," Jirina explained. "But someone had knocked her off—is that how you say it? Of course, they knew right away who'd done it, because this poor girl really did have a lover in the Central Committee, and all the ballerinas claimed he was a sado-masochist with tendencies towards necrophilia."

"Did they arrest him?"

Jirina responded by tapping her forehead again. I understood this time: obviously they'd had him declared insane.

She invited me to stay for supper and served me a caloric bomb she called "Spanish Birds"—probably her mistranslation, because it was really Mock Duck, starchy, greasy, and delicious. While we ate, she went on spinning her Czech yarns. They seem to be a form of oral literature, a response to the Czech need to escape reality.

The story of the chef at the Old English Pub is typical of the genre. It goes like this. The chef had been working on an ocean liner called something like the *Clematis Gottwald*, and when it docked in New York he "chose freedom", as Jirina put it. In other words, he jumped ship. Now, to be granted political asylum you have to demonstrate that you're a political refugee as the United Nations defines that term: someone who for political, religious, or racial reasons is persecuted so severely in his native land that he is unable to realize his full human potential. They hadn't started locking up chefs in Eastern Europe yet, the chef didn't believe in God, and he wasn't Jewish. Therefore he based his case solely on the lack of personal fulfilment. He testified that the state norms on food and nutrition (which applied even in extra-territorial waters) were so restrictive that they prevented him from fully developing his professional talents as a cook.

It wasn't a strong argument, but the judges finally ruled in his favour after hearing an eloquent plea from a woman who claimed to own a restaurant in Manhattan and promised to employ the chef immediately. The very next day the chef found himself working in a restaurant that was to ducks what Colonel Sanders is to chickens. The menu was simple:

Whole Roast Duck—$14.00
Half Roast Duck—$9.00
Quarter Roast Duck—$5.00

The prices varied, but never the menu.

When Herman Chumac found him, the chef was slowly going out of his mind over an endless procession of golden-brown Pope's Noses. The poor fellow was so distraught with boredom that he actually believed there were only two things he could do: return to Czechoslovakia or jump off the Brooklyn Bridge. Herman listened to his story and offered him a third choice: a job in Toronto.

The chef soon discovered that the Old English Pub's menu was pretty much the same as that on the ocean liner. But here there were no state-imposed norms, and so at last his creations attained world-class levels. And he liked it here.

"Does he really?" I asked Jirina. "What exactly does he like about the place?" I always feel a little uneasy when people who weren't born here get too enthusiastic about the country.

"A lot," replied Jirina. "There are things here which over *there*," and she pointed through the french doors where the morning sun was pouring into her kitchen, so I guess she meant in the east, "don't exist."

"Such as?"

"Such as the air."

Exiles are always exaggerating, I thought, so I said, "You mean there's less pollution here?"

"On the contrary. But here you don't notice the air when you breathe it."

I thought about that. Did I notice the air when I breathed? Certainly not. Breathing is a reflex activity, after all. "I think you're stringing me a line, Jirina," I said, but she explained that it was a kind of metaphor and said there was no point trying to explain because I wouldn't understand anyway. I'd had enough ridicule, so I dropped the matter.

"And so," I told Sheila, "the people who hang out at the Old English Pub are almost all Czechs. They drink enormous quantities of imported beer, spend most of their time arguing, and even get into fights."

"What over?" asked Sheila.

"Politics," I replied.

Sheila became alert. The light of deduction flashed in her eyes and her Irish freckles darkened. "Political disagreements?"

I nodded.

"What do they argue about?"

I did my best to pass on Jirina's explanation of the political conflicts within the Czech community in Toronto. I think it would be easier to describe everyday life in a wasps' nest.

The Czechs, it seems, are a very fractional lot. The two main groups are apparently the post-February and the post-August communities. At first I thought this had to do with the time of year the émigrés arrived in Canada, but Jirina explained that February refers to February 1948, when the Communists staged a coup in Prague, while August means August 1968, when the Russians invaded Czechoslovakia. On both occasions waves of people left the country and washed up on our shores. To make things even more complicated, the post-August bunch are apparently either ex-Communists or non-Communists, whereas the post-February crowd are all anti-Communists, and the latter believe the post-August non-Communists must in fact be crypto-Communists, or they couldn't have survived for so long under a Communist regime. There are further divisions and subdivisions—one of the strangest factions has to be the devotees of Franz Josef II, the last emperor in the Hapsburg Dynasty which ruled over the Austro-Hungarian Empire until it was dismantled in 1918. But I can't sort out all these groups, and their subtle distinctions are beyond me.

However, I should mention one peculiarity that stands out and in a way unifies this otherwise fragmented community: they all seem to believe there are secret agents of the Prague government among them, reporting back on their activities and sowing dissension among them. When I pointed out to Jirina that the RCMP would never allow this, she merely tapped her forehead again and gave me that annoyed, pitying look of hers.

That was all I could tell Sheila about the political complexities of the Canadian Czechs. It wasn't clear to me what any of it had to do with Heather's murder, but I was confident she'd assimilate the information and find a place for it in the hypothesis she appeared to be forming.

I was wrong. Sheila still felt instinctively that my sister's murder had been a crime of passion, because of the earlier incident in which the same man had severely injured Heather in a quarrel. As far as she was concerned, it was simply a matter of proving it.

I myself was uncertain. For my liking, there were altogether too many members of that argumentative and highly politicized group mixed up in the events.

2

Father and Daughter

Take Sheila's secretary, for example. Her name is Sue McLaughlin and her husband, Mack, is in Vietnam. He's been decorated several times for bravery and he's been wounded twice. Although Sheila considers draft dodgers to be heroes, whereas men who stay in the army and fight are in her opinion cowards because they don't have the guts to stand up to the Yankee government, she sees the wives of both as victims of an unjust American war. In fact, Sue owes her job to her coward of a husband, since Sheila picked her from about a dozen candidates. After Sue explained that she had the first of her two daughters while she was still unmarried, and left the father "because he was an idiot, but Mack doesn't mind", the job was definitely hers. Sheila sees unwed mothers as the highest category of competence.

Sue's real name is Zuzana, and she comes from Prague. She became a U.S. citizen by marrying the son of an American couple who were expelled from Czechoslovakia for political reasons. After Mack was sent to Vietnam she and her two children moved up to Canada so Sue could care for her father, who had somehow landed in Toronto. The fact that Sue didn't leave until some time after the Russian invasion would normally have made her even more attractive to Sheila, but since hiring her Sheila had met several Czech refugees who talked like ultra-rightists. When one of them told her that Goebbels was a good socialist too, she concluded that although the Russian invasion had had a negative effect on the majority of the people as individuals, it had collectively benefited the politically most advanced minority because it had forestalled the imminent collapse of socialism.

"And where do you stand?" she had asked the secretary, for as soon as the truth about Sue's background came out, Sheila began to probe the girl's opinions. After all, her father-in-law, hounded from America by McCarthy, had been so swayed by the revisionists in Prague that he had actually gone back to the headwaters of capitalism.

"What do you mean, 'stand'?" the Czech girl had asked. She was nervous, perhaps because the conversation was turning into something more like an interrogation.

"I mean politically. Are you a socialist?"

"Maybe," replied Sue evasively. "My father is, anyway."

"But you aren't?"

"I don't know," said Sue matter-of-factly.

"How can you not know? Either you are or you aren't."

"I don't know whether I am or not. I just think people have the right to live decent lives."

"And don't people lead decent lives where you come from?"

"You mean in the States?"

"No, in Czechoslovakia."

"How can they live decent lives without freedom?"

Sheila always reacted angrily when she heard that word. With undisguised irony, she said, "In Canada, only those who can afford it are free."

"Really?" said the secretary, who was making $250 a week, gross. "I guess I'm one of the lucky ones, then."

Sheila gave the elegantly dressed young woman a rapid perusal. Sue had claimed that her clothes came from the Salvation Army: the skirt, a dollar; the velvet jacket, two.

"But don't you think the rich enjoy far more freedom than you do?"

"That's true everywhere," replied the secretary.

Sheila was nonplussed. Surely, she reasoned, there can be no rich people under socialism. In any case, Sheila had been taught that humanity would never attain complete equality and social justice, either sexually or economically, until it achieved true socialism, so she began to appeal to the future.

"And doesn't that bother you?"

"Well—maybe I'll be rich one day too. When Mack finishes graduate school. But I doubt it. With his profession—palaeontology?" and she wrinkled her nose. "But I don't mind it when people are well off. The main thing is that the poor aren't humiliated."

And having uttered this strange opinion, the secretary sat down at her typewriter, put on the dictaphone headset, and energetically began to type. Sheila retreated into her own office and, beneath a Judy Chicago poster and portraits of Gloria Steinem and Germaine Greer (not long before, there had been portraits of Mao Tse Tung and Enver Hoxha), she spent two hours and eight ounces of rye trying to fathom the girl's strange ideology. She concluded that, whatever it was, it wasn't socialist.

But because Sheila was a decent person at heart, she reminded herself that Sue was new here and still bewitched by the absurd affluence of the capitalist marketplace, and by the marble banks where the staff are polite even to bricklayers, regardless of how little they have in their accounts—but then, of course, Sheila had no idea how much bricklayers had in their accounts. Her own balance was of a rather different magnitude. And because she had a kind heart, she resolved to try, with patience, to bring her secretary around to the correct way of thinking.

She came back into the front office where Sue was working industriously over her IBM Selectric, offered her a cigarette, and asked her in a kindly way why she was living with her father in Toronto when her husband's family was in Memphis, Tennessee.

What she learned erased for ever the poor impression left by the secretary's political immaturity. As far as Sheila was concerned, this attractive girl with the green eyes carried about with her the aura of an inherited heroism.

It turned out that Sue's father was no ordinary immigrant, but had fled to Canada in the final stage of his escape from prison.

Sheila's heart was always on the side of convicts. Their crimes mattered little to her because she believed that whatever they did was a result of their social background. Long prison sentences and lack of fibre in the prison diet outraged her. She considered every prisoner a soul-brother, with the possible exception of the rapist.

"How did he manage to escape?" she asked respectfully.

"He won't talk about it," Sue replied. "The thing is, they put his—well, his girlfriend—in prison. She's a singer, her name is Eve Adam. This happened after he made it out of the country, because she'd been seen a couple of times in the company of that writer. They—"

"Who?"

"The secret police. They were following him. The writer, I mean. But they couldn't go after him directly because he was a foreigner and he was famous, so they locked her up instead. But Dad doesn't want to talk about how she helped him escape. He says exiles talk too much and word would get back to Prague and they'd put another five years at least on her sentence. You see, Eve travelled abroad quite a bit and she made lots of—well, acquaintances—in her travels. One of them was this writer. He's very famous but the main reason why she chose him for the job was because he looks a lot like Father. He's got blue eyes and a round face, and he's very much against *them*. So he agreed.''

The plan was well worked out. The elderly English writer was so famous, Sue said, that the secret police probably wouldn't have dared to do anything even if the plot had been discovered. The writer flew to Prague as a guest of the Writers' Union. This caused a certain amount of consternation among his friends in the West, for it was generally known that the union toadied up to the Russian government and that several of its former members, now expelled, were sitting in prison. But the famous writer made no attempt to justify himself. He was wined and dined by the Ministry of Culture and he even visited a dacha—a kind of country estate made available by the government to its officially recognized writers as a reward for not writing. At least, that's how Sue put it, and Sheila didn't question her. Finally the writer allowed himself to be interviewed by the Communist Party daily. Sue said he managed to speak in generalities about trivial things like world peace (Sheila, though she wondered what was trivial about world peace, didn't interrupt) but it didn't matter, Sue said, because all they cared about was having his name in the paper. If he spoke in empty banalities, so much the better.

And then, when the writer was at the airport ready to leave, he discovered that he had lost both his passport and his air ticket to Canada, where he was flying to visit a sister.

The day before, immigration officials in Montreal had picked up and held a man carrying an English passport issued for someone with an English name and listing his profession as a writer. The man could barely speak English but the exasperated official—who disliked speaking anything but French—gathered that he was asking for political asylum. When they probed further, they discovered that the man only superficially resembled the photograph in his passport, and when questioned about that, he readily admitted to having found the passport and used it to leave his country, Czechoslovakia. The officials wanted to know why and he admitted, once again without being tortured, that he had just escaped from prison in Prague. So the RCMP locked him up and reported the affair to the Czechoslovakian embassy. The ambassador himself flew in from Ottawa for a confrontation with the prisoner, who stuck to his story. The famous writer in Prague stuck to his story as well. He was a *very* famous writer, and in two weeks he was to attend the congress of an important literary society in New York where they were expecting official delegates from Prague. The Prague police therefore agreed to accept the story about the lost passport. But they arrested the refugee's mistress, who had been observed rather frequently in the famous writer's company, and she was charged with a currency offence and sent to prison for fifteen years. The writer left the country on a temporary passport issued by the British embassy and there was pressure to turn the prisoner in Canada over to Interpol.

Then the Czech mafia stepped in. A family in Chicago gave a statement to the American press claiming that the refugee— who turned out to be a former police lieutenant—had helped their little girl escape from Czechoslovakia and rejoin them. The Czechoslovak Association of Canada hired an experienced immigration lawyer and the *Toronto Sun* launched an energetic campaign against the impending extradition. In the middle of all this, a seventy-five-year-old Czech professor of North American history died in Prague of a brain haemorrhage after a sixteen-hour interrogation by the police. The professor had received an OBE after the Second World War for aid rendered to Canadian prisoners of war (for which he had barely escaped death in Buchenwald) and had had an honorary degree from Queen's University. To make matters worse, the prime minister had just signed a long-term agreement with the Soviet Union which was very unpopular and which many people believed carried a lot of hidden conditions with it. In other words, the situation was hopelessly tangled up in political complexities. After a few weeks of tense negotiations, Prague decided to release the refugee from prison *post factum* for good behaviour after having served a third of his sentence, and even that was antedated so that his escape would appear to fall at the end of the first third. And Canada granted the man landed-immigrant status. Now he was working as a parking-lot attendant next to a big Loblaws store on Bloor Street.

From there, the man sent two questions to us the next day, via his daughter: "Why wasn't Mrs. McCavish at home that evening? And did anyone know she wouldn't be?"

Odd questions from a parking-lot attendant. Sheila was intrigued by the line of reasoning implied, though, and she said she wanted to meet this former detective before going to talk to Jirina.

It was a stifling hot August afternoon in Toronto, the kind you dream about in January and then can't wait to escape when it finally arrives. Air conditioners were humming in apartment windows but there was none in the tiny attendant's booth at the edge of the parking lot, and the attendant himself was perspiring profusely. Crowds of shoppers were pouring out of the supermarket carrying fistfuls of plastic bags stuffed with brightly packaged junk food. Sights like this always depressed Sheila. One of her earlier crusades had been against processed foods, and I could still remember her histrionic question: what would be the life-span of these poor consumers of frozen food and chemically improved delicacies, with their labels that read like recipes for slow death by poisoning? I had tried to point out that the life expectancy of these unfortunates was rising by the year, but she managed to ignore the statistics.

I looked at the man in the parking booth. He was a thinnish man with a large, round face that looked rather like a pink moon. He was almost bald except for a tuft of unruly hair at the back of his head. Flanking his button nose (it was obvious where Sue had inherited hers) were two glistening forget-me-not eyes— eyes that appeared innocent, perhaps even somewhat naive. But the most remarkable thing of all was the deep melancholy that radiated from them.

For a former detective, Mr. Boruvka didn't exactly look like a genius.

"He could have been wearing gloves," he said. "That would explain why there are no fingerprints."

"In August?" objected Sheila. "In this heat?"

"I beg your pardon," Mr. Boruvka said politely, "but that would indicate premeditation."

"But how do we know he went there with the intention of killing her?" Sheila wondered. "Crimes of passion are almost always committed without premeditation."

"I don't know." The former detective turned to take parking money from a statuesque black woman with a bawling little girl who had hurt her mouth trying to stick an inhumanly large sucker into it. "I once had a case like it in Italy, and there were no fingerprints there either. The murderer had worn gloves, of course."

Sheila disagreed. "We already know he was there at the time of the murder, and his fingerprints are on the door, even though they're only on the outside. And the main thing is that he had a very good motive, and he's already demonstrated that he can lose his self-control."

"Of course you are right," said Mr. Boruvka awkwardly. "But there is still the matter of those missing fingerprints."

"Given all we know about Heather," Sheila said, "can you imagine any *other* motive one might have had for murdering her?" Sheila caught herself. "I'm sorry, Neil."

"Don't worry about it," I reassured her. Perhaps it was the sudden activity, but the more I concentrated on the job of bringing her murderer to justice, the less I thought about Heather.

"You are right," admitted the melancholy parking-lot attendant for the second time. "I know almost nothing about her. But this motivation you mention—excuse me, but, well, I would still like very much to know the answers to my questions."

3

Who Knew about Heather?

"Him a detective?" said Sheila, slamming the car door. "As a detective he makes a good parking-lot attendant!"

We bad-mouthed the former detective as we drove to Jirina's house in my BMW. But when we arrived in that deceptively charming little Cabbagetown cul-de-sac and I introduced them, the first thing Sheila asked Jirina was why she hadn't been home the evening my kid sister was murdered. Obviously she didn't think the question was entirely irrelevant.

"I've already told the police everything I know," said the editor of *Toronto Lady*. "It was just that I had to go to Kitchener." And she stroked the brindled tomcat, which had settled comfortably in her lap. The cat dozed blissfully. It had been the only eye-witness to my sister's unhappy end. I was sorry it hadn't been a bulldog.

"Any particular reason for going there?"

"To pick up a manuscript," said the editor. "At three o'clock that day I got a call from—well, it doesn't matter who from. It was someone from Prague visiting her daughter in Kitchener. She'd managed to smuggle a manuscript out of Czechoslovakia for me. She said she was going back to Prague the next morning.

They always leave things like that till the last minute." And Jirina sighed. "She was visiting her daughter for two months, but she was so upset about her little grandchild that she forgot about the manuscript until she started packing."

"Did something happen to the grandchild?" I asked.

"Oh no. But she couldn't talk to the brat because the brat only speaks English."

"Why didn't she just mail you the manuscript?" asked Sheila.

"She has a thing about using the mails."

"I can understand that. They're hardly reliable."

"That's not the reason. It would take me a long time to explain and then," said Jirina, casting an experienced eye over my girl and glancing at me, "you'd think I was exaggerating."

I could tell that these two young women would probably not get on very well. Sheila began asking questions in the same tone she had used when interrogating Sue on matters of freedom.

"What was so important about the manuscript?"

"That's just it. It wasn't important at all. I'd already got it from another source. But I didn't know that when she called. She didn't want to tell me what it was about over the phone."

"And you stayed there overnight?" Sheila asked. "Kitchener's just a couple of hours' drive. If the messenger called you at three, and you left—"

"About four. But it took me ages to find a hotel because the Knights of Columbus were having a convention. Then I remembered that the manager of the Savoy is a Czech, someone called Trcka. I don't know him personally but he subscribes to my newspaper. And they found a free room for me, even though Trcka was away on business."

"But why did you stay overnight in the first place? If you got to Kitchener by half-past five or so, you could have left at seven and been back in Toronto before nine."

Jirina looked down at the cat in her lap and said nothing for a moment. "I wish to God I had come back," she said finally, and looked at me. Her eyes were sad. "But the fact is, I hate driving. It really tires me out, and dusk is the worst time of day. Anyway, I wanted to have a good chat with the lady from Prague. In the end—and this so often happens—the messenger turned out to be more useful than the manuscript she was bringing. Her younger daughter used to go with the son of a very big *apparatchik* and she told me—"

And Jirina spun us another unlikely yarn of scandal and intrigue among the ruling class in Prague. It seems that the very big *apparatchik* was having an affair with a prominent pop singer. His wife caught them *in flagrante* in a government dacha, chased them both naked into a nearby lake, and they emerged a few hundred yards down the shore at a Young Pioneers' camp. Not recognizing the big *apparatchik* without his medals on, the camp leaders held the two of them at bay with pitchforks while someone went for the police.

"The best thing about the story," Jirina went on, "is that it was the man's own son, who's a follower of Trotsky and is anxious to bring the Party into disrepute, who tipped off his mother about the affair. And there was a scandal, but the boy underestimated the power of the People to put a lid on matters like that."

"Is that the kind of stuff you print in *Toronto Lady*?" asked Sheila incredulously. "I had the impression from Neil it was a cultural and political—" And she stopped. "Come to think of it," she went on after a pause, "I suppose that *would* interest the ladies of Toronto."

"The interest isn't limited to the ladies of Toronto," Jirina replied. "At least two hundred copies of each issue get to Prague through various channels. Of course, it isn't just the ladies of Prague who read it. I have certain other readers who are far more interested in how I get all this exciting stuff out of Prague in the first place."

The sun was slipping behind the high towers of St. James Town. A ray of sunlight entered the room and fell upon a strange, elongated nude on the wall that looked as though it were lying behind a row of prisms. The cat on Jirina's lap opened its eyes and I caught a brief flash of emerald; then it turned to stare at its mistress, its little pink nose pointing towards the ceiling. "Miaow," it said, gazing with feline steadfastness at Jirina's face.

"Have you told all this to the police?" I asked.

"Well—not all of it, no," she admitted.

"Why not?"

"It's a kind of conditioned reflex left over from Czechoslovakia. Whenever a policeman asks me about anything, my mind goes blank," she said, touching the cat's pink nose with a brown finger.

I began to feel that we were getting, and would continue to get, far more out of her than Bill Kendrick had managed to do.

"Who knew you wouldn't be coming home that evening?" asked Sheila after a pause.

"I don't think anyone did," said Jirina. "Heather must have known, of course, because she could read the message I left on the mirror."

I had an idea. "Were you aware that my sister had invited Herman Chumac to spend the night with her at your place?"

Jirina's eyes narrowed and she paused before she spoke. "How could I be? I'd already left by the time Heather came. She had her own key. She used to sleep at my place whenever she needed...." Jirina stopped, but I knew what she'd been about to say. Heather had lived with our father, so she had often needed another place to go. I nodded and Jirina continued, "Hold on, there is someone else who knew I wouldn't be at home. Werner von Vogeltanz. He was supposed to come to supper, but I called his secretary to cancel the invitation."

The cat lowered its head and closed its eyes again as the editor of *Toronto Lady* scratched behind its ears.

"Who's he?" asked Sheila.

"He's the director of Austriacraft, Incorporated," said Jirina. "It's an import-export firm that deals in baroque beer steins and little porcelain boys in lederhosen. Most of it's sentimental kitsch, but there's a huge market for it here. Vogeltanz is originally from Austria, but he's been in Canada for years. I met him in the Old English Pub, where all the old supporters of the Austro-Hungarian Empire get together. Vogeltanz is one of those who believes they should have left the empire intact. He claims it would have provided a perfect buffer zone against the Russians. He's a very bright man," she sighed, "and quite good-looking in his own way."

Sheila didn't bother to ask why Jirina had invited this man for supper, probably because she assumed it was for the most natural of reasons. Her notions of Jirina were understandably stereotypical, for the editor of the glossy tabloid looked like a widow who was, on the whole, very merry indeed.

4

What I Didn't Tell Sheila

I wasn't as well acquainted with all my poor sister's friends as Harrison Morrison was, but I couldn't recall any Austrian aristocrat, although it was possible they had known each other. Among my sister's many weaknesses—like cocaine, older men, exotic lovers, and horseback riding—was a fascination with aristocracy. At least six pictures of Prince Charles—one of them showing him in swimming trunks—hung on her bedroom wall, and I don't think it was just his looks that appealed to her. I reasoned that she would not have overlooked a gentleman with a name like Werner von Vogeltanz.

We found his name in the telephone directory and dialled the number. A voice answered: "This is Mr. von Vogeltanz's residence. Mr. von Vogeltanz cannot come to the telephone at the moment, but...."

The voice on the answering machine spoke perfect English with a slight hint of what could have been a German accent. I left a message asking him to call me back.

It was late when I finally drove Sheila home. She was exhausted. This was her first big case, and when she kissed me good night it wasn't much more than a mechanical peck on the cheek.

She didn't invite me to stay. I walked her to the door, climbed back in the car, and headed for my father's place.

I had been living with my father temporarily while my house was renovated, and now that Heather was dead, my father would be glad to have me there to ease him through his grief. Dad was retired and had nothing to do but brood.

The sun had set and Toronto was aglow. The bright, downtown office towers threw their radiance into the warm night air, and the CN Tower was blinking against the black, velvet sky. I was fond of the city and the thought that my sister was no longer here to enjoy it made me feel wretched. I tried to recall the details of the life she had been determined to live so intensely. It was like watching a very short film. I hoped she had at least enjoyed herself.

Then, for some reason, I thought of Sue, the former detective's daughter. Did she enjoy life? I knew her husband had gone to Prague as a small child when his family had left the U.S.A. to escape the long shadow cast by Senator McCarthy. Then something had happened, either to them or to Prague, because they had been expelled on forty-eight hours' notice in the early seventies. Whatever it was, the McLaughlins went back to Memphis, Tennessee. No sooner had they arrived, however, than the American government took Sue's husband off to Vietnam. His photograph—in uniform, to Sheila's displeasure—stood on Sue's desk. What chance had Sue had to enjoy her life? What chance had my little sister had? Yet here was Sue, bravely unscathed, though her life had been surrounded by violence. And here was my little sister—raised in the quiet and uneventful streets of Rosedale, lacking nothing, pampered, confused, hungry for life—and now, far from the battlefields of the world, she was dead. Why her?

The night lights of Toronto became blurred. I reached for my handkerchief, blew my nose, then turned north. In five minutes I was home.

A short time later I was rummaging around in my father's desk, looking for the most recent telephone bill; there was something I wanted to check. It didn't take me long to find what I was looking for. The call I had in mind had been made late at night about two weeks before and there was only one item on the bill with the full night-time discount. A quick check with directory assistance revealed that the number belonged to the Savoy Hotel in Kitchener.

It was too late to drive to Kitchener. But there was a potential well of information about the Czechs right here in Toronto. Fifteen minutes later, I pulled up in front of the Old English Pub.

The restaurant was filled with the very un-English odour of a culinary abomination called *sauerbraten*. Jirina once foisted *sauerbraten* on me and that night I understood for the first time why they refer to certain types of gastric distress as "heartburn".

The only English I heard in the place came from the lips of a Chinese waitress who asked me in a flawless Toronto accent if I'd like to eat. I told her what I wanted and she guided me past a table where a boisterous group of middle-aged men were drinking beer from what looked like an enormous glass boot. As far as I could tell, they were speaking German. Naturally, everyone was eating *sauerbraten*.

I walked into the manager's office and Herman Chumac, who was sitting at his desk, jumped to his feet, almost knocking over a drink that was on the blotting pad. He was holding a large red handkerchief to his face and had evidently just been blowing his nose. He quickly thrust the handkerchief into his pocket, revealing a nose that was almost as red as the material. Perhaps he'd been crying. His nose was—strange. Battered, shapeless— well, hard to describe. It drew attention to itself in an otherwise ordinary, slightly puffy face framed with slightly greying sideburns and topped by a shiny billiard-ball of a pate. His body, however, was tall and solid and muscular. Under normal circumstances he might have been intimidating but at the moment there was nothing arrogant about him at all. I couldn't tell whether it was fear or sadness in his eyes.

"Mr. Donby—I'm sorry, I wasn't expecting...."

"That's all right," I replied, as brusquely as I could. "I've come to talk about Heather."

"Surely you don't believe I—"

"I don't know, but I'd certainly like to get at the truth."

"I understand, Mr. Donby. You have my word of honour that I had nothing to do with this tragic business."

I looked around the office. It was lined with dark wood panelling. English hunting scenes hung at regular intervals on the panels and directly behind his desk, looking like Mickey Mouse among the Elgin Marbles, was an ostentatious cartoon of a fat man in an old-fashioned army uniform holding a foaming stein of yellow beer. Below it were the words: Take It Easy!

There was a pungent haze in the room that made my eyes sting, and when I glanced at his desk I saw the source: a huge ashtray brimming with cigar butts. Herman saw what I was looking at and, as though he were alarmed, his hand shot into his breast pocket. He pulled out a metal object that flashed in the dim light, and held it towards me. It was a silver cigar case. I don't smoke Churchills, so I pulled out my own case—a gift, I realized painfully, from Heather—and took out a Havana. Then I laid the case on the table and sat down. If he's going to tell me all he knows, I thought, one cigar won't be enough.

The trembling hand, still extended, sank to the table and I heard a metallic snap.

I lit my cigar. I don't know why I smoke them. I don't like the taste. But when I exhale the thick smoke, letting it escape slowly from my mouth, I feel touched by the larger mysteries of existence.

I blew out a thick cloud of smoke and for a moment Herman's face and his unfortunate nose vanished behind it.

"I've been thinking," I said slowly, "that perhaps someone else is mixed up in this."

"If you mean someone else did it," said Herman, "then of course they did." He seemed to catch himself and stopped. "Who else do you think could have done it?"

"I've heard your alibi," I said.

"Who told you?"

"Let's just say I'm taking an active interest in the case," I replied. "Frankly, I've wondered about you ever since you took a swipe at Heather."

"I know, Mr. Donby, I know," said Herman uneasily. "I was extremely fond of your sister, believe me. But she was—she was difficult sometimes. I did love her, though."

"I don't suppose you were the only one who found her difficult." I took another puff on my cigar. "Suppose we assume it was someone else who did it."

"It *was* someone else, Mr. Donby." He fell silent.

"Any thoughts about who it might be? Was Heather mixed up in something I don't know about? Did she have any enemies, any—unsavoury obligations?"

"Mr. Donby," Herman began. "I knew your sister well—and apart from a few expensive habits, which I assure you I was trying to break her of, she was a very nice, sweet girl. She had admirers, yes, but no enemies that I know of. Believe me, if I knew of anything that might help track down her killer, I'd be the first to—"

"Do you know the manager of the Savoy Hotel in Kitchener?"

Herman shot me a quick, quizzical look. "Not personally. His name is Dusan Trcka."

The way he pronounced it, the name sounded like a wet sparkler on Dominion Day. "A countryman of yours?"

"Yes."

"And you say you don't know him personally?" I said with sticky emphasis.

"I give you my word of honour."

He was making too many appeals to honour to satisfy me. "You don't happen to know if he knew Heather?"

He shook his head.

"Can't you even tell me something about him that might give me a lead?"

"All I know is, they say he's an aristocrat. There is an old Czech noble family by that name, dating way back, but—"

I abruptly exhaled a great cloud of smoke. Bonnie Prince Charlie in a bathing suit. Von Vogeltanz. And now another blueblood. Herman's eyes were avoiding my gaze. I said nothing, but watched him closely. Then I blew another cloud of smoke directly into his face.

I glanced at the cartoon on the wall. "Take It Easy!" I supposed that was good advice, but there are some situations in which not even a powerfully built fifty-year-old can bring himself to be completely at ease.

"You've given me something to think about," I said, picking up my cigar case from the desk. And without saying goodbye I walked out of the room, leaving him to stew in his own juice.

My sister may not have known Dusan Trcka, but I'll never forget the midnight conversation she had with someone at his hotel in Kitchener. I'd picked up my bedside extension to call Sheila and found myself eavesdropping on an impassioned argument. At least, my sister sounded upset. The man on the other end— she called him "lover", but then she called every male over eighteen that—was considerably calmer. Heather had obviously had what they call an emotional involvement with him—that much I understood—but the gist of the conversation was that he was dropping her and she didn't want to be dropped. Heather used every trick of female rhetoric at her command, but the man remained unmoved, at least until the end, when he suddenly exploded. "Look here, Heather, it's past midnight, I've got an important meeting tomorrow, and if you want to know the truth, I've had enough. It's been fun, but you're a real bitch and I'd advise you to watch what you do in the future. Goodbye." And there was a sharp click in the receiver.

The unknown man, who had a slight accent, might simply have been a guest at the hotel. But there were surprising coincidences in the case. On the night of her death, my little sister's Czech lover had been poking around a house belonging to a Czech editor who that very night had had to go to Kitchener where she'd stayed in a hotel run by a Czech manager, the same hotel that Heather had called a couple of weeks before and had a violent argument with a man who spoke with a foreign accent. Was he Czech as well? There were already far too many of them on the merry-go-round.

And then there was the former detective. He was also Czech, and he'd asked who had known Mrs. McCavish wouldn't be at home that night.

Jirina is a talkative woman, probably even more so in her own language among her compatriots than she is with me. She had checked into the Savoy Hotel around half past six on the day of the murder. You can drive from Kitchener to Toronto along Highway 401 in an hour and a half—less, if you are driven by forces other than horsepower. Herman had knocked on Mrs. McCavish's door after ten p.m. By that time, my sister was already dead. And the man with a name like a wet sparkler was out of town that evening on a "business trip".

If it was he, how had he learned that my sister would be alone?

I also recalled Jirina's admission that she had told Bill Kendrick and the police much less than she had told Sheila and me. That could mean that the police didn't know about Trcka. And I had certainly forgotten to tell them about my sister's midnight phone call.

When I arrived at the Savoy Hotel in Kitchener just before noon the next day, the manager was off on another business trip and the only physical trace of his presence was a framed photograph over the bar with a shiny brass plaque below it bearing the legend: DUSAN TRCKA, MANAGER, WELCOMES YOU TO THE SAVOY.

Trcka might well be an aristocrat. As far as I could tell from the photograph, which had been amply retouched and airbrushed, he had proud features and a prominent, aquiline nose, slightly oversized but all the more aristocratic for that. The hair around his temples was a fashionable silver grey and, like Herman, he appeared to be on the wrong side of fifty. Thus my sister had at least two reasons for being attracted to him. The photo, in full colour, revealed that the master of the Savoy had steely grey eyes. His smile was the wide, confident grin of optimistic businessmen everywhere, displaying a magnificent set of teeth. It was impossible to tell whether they were the work of God or of man.

I sat down at a small table in the dimly lit bar and ordered a double Glenfiddich on the rocks. The bartender may well have concluded that I was a lush, for it was scarcely noon. I had a brief vision of sitting with Sheila in more agreeable climes, somewhere on the Côte du Soleil, far from the aura of guilt and shame that still clings to daytime drinking here.

After a few moments had gone by and my eyes had grown accustomed to the gloom, I realized I wasn't alone. Two tables away, over a glass of sherry, sat another early drinker, an elderly man dressed in a neatly cut but slightly old-fashioned suit that looked as though it had been made to measure in Savile Row just after the First World War. In his lapel, like the prime minister, he wore a fresh red rose.

At first I paid little attention to him because I was still studying the photograph of the grinning aristocrat, as though the gaudy colours and expert retouching could yield up some awful secret about my little sister and her unfortunate attraction to older men. Once, when I asked her about it in anger, she retorted that older men knew all about life, whereas wimps like me could give her nothing but bad advice. Her response outraged me, but recently I'd begun to understand more of what was behind her clichéed insults. Heather had a powerful desire to know and grasp life at some deeper level than the superficial understanding offered by her peers. The way she chose to attain this knowledge was wrong, perhaps, and in the end it may have destroyed her. Essentially, however, that was all she wanted—to know life. But how could she possibly learn anything worth knowing from this grinning toothpaste ad?

"Sir?" a grave and gloomy voice beside me said.

I turned around. It was the man with the rose in his lapel. I stared at him more closely. If anyone looked like a nobleman around here, this old gentleman did. He had a distinctively English air about him, like someone out of a *Punch* cartoon, with a little grey moustache under his nose and a real gold pince-nez perched on top of it. His eyes were full of baleful self-absorption, like a basset hound. The only things out of place were his hands: they were large and gnarled, as though he had worked with them all his life.

"Do you know His Excellency?" he asked. It sounded like a question from beyond the grave.

"Do you mean Tr—that man in the picture?" I replied.

He nodded. "Count Trcka."

"Count Tr—"

He nodded again and, with a thick finger that might have been crippled with gout, pointed to something standing next to the vodka bottles behind the bar. "His coat of arms," he announced.

I got up and walked over to the bar to take a closer look. Sure enough, it was a plaque displaying a coat of arms with some creature—it could have been a hoot-owl—balancing what looked like a soccer ball on its head. There was a bar dividing the shield in half diagonally and a golden crown in the upper corner with points like a sheriff's star.

"His Excellency is executive secretary of our heraldic society," said the old gentleman.

I came back, sat down, and looked with interest at this strange creature. He was just crossing his legs, and as he did so I caught sight of a pair of genuine spats. The crease in his trousers was razor-sharp.

"Allow me to introduce myself," he said, holding out his hand ceremoniously. "I am Rupert, King of Bohemia."

The sensation I experienced can only be described as mystical. Since taking over Jirina's portfolio, I had grown used to meeting a lot of Czechs, some of whom made impossible claims about themselves—emboldened, no doubt, by the virtual impossibility of anyone ever checking up on them. This was the first time I had ever met one who claimed royalty.

I braced myself for another wild yarn by draining my glass; this brought the underworked bartender to my side almost at once. "The same, sir?" he asked, and then looked at the old gentleman's glass. "And for you, Your Majesty?"

No, I wasn't hallucinating. I offered to buy the king a drink and he accepted without hesitation. He dipped his moustache in a fresh glass of sherry and, wiping it off with a finger that bore a huge signet ring with a two-tailed lion on it, said, "You must think I'm mad."

"Of course not, of course not," I said, too eagerly.

"Ah, but you do," he replied. "That's understandable. A Czech king in Canada does not sound very plausible, I agree. But that's not the whole of it. At the present time, I am also the rightful pretender to the Grand Duchy of Canada. Are you familiar at all with Canadian history?"

"Well," I said uneasily, "I took a couple of courses when I was at university."

The monarch and pretender nodded dismissively. "This land was originally called Prince Rupert's Land. Do you know who Prince Rupert was?"

It had never occurred to me to ask. I had always thought of him as a piece of territory, like Mr. Baffin. Unlike my sister, I had never taken much interest in royalty.

"Prince Rupert was the legal and rightful heir to the Czech throne. He was born in Prague but he had to flee the country with his father at the age of one when the Austrian Hapsburgs usurped the Czech kingdom after the Battle of the White Mountain in 1620. Rupert's father was Frederick the Winter King, the last of the legitimate Czech monarchs."

This was the second time in two days that the Hapsburgs had been mentioned in conversation. They must have been quite a family.

"Historians have established," the old man went on, punctuating his monologue with noisy sips of sherry, "that Prince Rupert never completely forgot the Czech he learned from his nanny. His mother, Elizabeth Stuart, was the daughter of James I, and therefore his Royal Brittanic Majesty, as compensation for Prince Rupert's lost kingdom of Bohemia, granted him a fiefdom which turned out to be a new territory discovered not long before on the other side of the Atlantic Ocean. This territory was owned by the Hudson's Bay Company, of which Prince Rupert was a founding member, and that land is now part of the Dominion of Canada. They called it Prince Rupert's Land, after the prince. That is the legal basis of my claim both to this continent and to the title I bear."

The barman did his job well and the room began to fill up with fog while the old man droned on in what was unmistakably a flat, mid-Ontario honk. With each new Glenfiddich I found his story more and more outrageous, and afterwards I was able to recall only its crude outlines. It seems that the man who claimed to be king was a retired farmer from Orangeville, and that Count Trcka had been the first to put him on the trail of his ancestors. Trcka had told him that it was a tradition in the Bohemian royal family to call first-born sons by the old-fashioned name of Rupert. Trcka had then agreed to help him trace his ancestry if he would join the Heraldic Society and pay the necessary research fee; the king, whose sons had both emigrated to Western Australia, agreed; and after a great deal of research that included several trips to Europe by the executive secretary, the Orangeville farmer had been presented with a regal set of roots. Trcka had discovered that according to an ancient medieval custom, the monarch's family name contained an acronym or palindrome that proved his claim to the throne of Bohemia. The core of the palindrome was the German word "von", but since the last two rightful kings of Bohemia had in fact been Germans, the chief of the Heraldic Society deemed there to be nothing wrong in this.

"And what is your surname, Your Majesty?" I asked, talking in the general direction of the rose.

"Novack. We've been in this country for three generations."

When his name was read backwards, the acronym was revealed: "kcavon". Trcka had explained to the king that the letters k.c.a. were a transposition of the Czech initials c.a.k., which stood for "Caesar and King", a form of address used since the fourteenth century for Czech rulers. The "von" simply indicated that the noble ancestry of the last *rex Bohemorum* originated in the Holy Roman Empire of the German nation. That, combined with the Christian name Rupert, which was a tradition in the Novack family....

During an interval, when the king had gone to the washroom and the waiter had left the bar for a moment, I put enough money on the table to cover the bill—both mine and the sovereign's— and walked to the bar. I pocketed a glossy publicity brochure bearing Trcka's photograph and strode quickly, if none too steadily, out of the hotel.

The glare and the heat of the day engulfed me like a tropical sea but I made it to the car and drove carefully back to the 401, pausing on the way at a small truck stop for a strong coffee and a hamburger. I also made a phone call to Sheila and asked her to check on something for me. While I was waiting for the woman to bring my order, I tried to force my mind, numbed by alcohol and still buzzing with the absurd monarch's hypnotic tale, into some semblance of rational activity.

I concluded that the tipsy divertimento with the unfortunate farmer from Orangeville had not been entirely a waste of time. In the first place, it put Trcka, whoever he was, in a dubious light. It was clear to me that long before Mr. Novack was restored to his throne, he would be plucked clean of the assets he had accumulated over a lifetime of hard work. More to the point, I had also learned that this Heraldic Society of which Trcka was executive secretary was supposed to have had its regular monthly meeting in the Savoy Hotel the very night Heather had been killed. About three o'clock that same afternoon, the king had been advised by telephone that the meeting had been cancelled because Count Trcka had been called away from Kitchener on urgent family business.

This fitted perfectly into the hypothesis that was beginning to emerge in my mind.

5

Mr. Boruvka's Past

Werner von Vogeltanz hadn't been in his office that morning.
Sue had left a message with his secretary, but when I got back to
Sheila's office that afternoon he still hadn't returned the call.

But someone was waiting in the agency. He was in a chair set
aside for clients, with his back to me, but I recognized at once
the unruly tuft of hair that not even the greasiest hair oil could
have tamed.

Mr. Boruvka.

Sheila was sitting at her desk, a furrow of distrust between
her eyes, wearing a sensational white summer dress with bare
shoulders and back. I was encouraged because here was another
subtle indication that she was mellowing out of her radical
feminist phase. I still recall with horror the mercifully brief era of
home-made sartorial creativity, inspired more by Dogpatch than
by New York, London, or Paris. Going to dinner in a restaurant
where the head waiter won't let you in without a tie, in the
company of a woman wrapped in a burlap sack, is like going
to a wedding in a boiler suit. True, Sheila was never denied
admittance; she looked too much like Daisy Mae for that. Still,
the glances we got from head waiters and ladies who looked

as though they shopped at Creeds made me feel naked in a briar patch. Sheila, however, would sit proudly at a table in a corner behind a pillar (they always seated us as much out of the way as possible; once a waiter even erected a Spanish screen to quarantine us from the rest of the clientele). To make matters worse, she would insist on smoking a gigantic cigar. The only other person in the world who smokes one that big is Fidel Castro.

Time, as it will, had swept all that away. Now she was sitting there in a pretty dress from a Yorkville boutique, listening to Mr. Boruvka, her brow knit in skepticism.

"I am afraid, Miss Sullivan," the detective was saying, "that I may have put you on the wrong road, without meaning to, with my questions."

"Wasn't it logical?" replied Sheila. "If it was a premeditated act, as you thought, then of course the murderer must have known Mrs. McCavish wouldn't be at home."

I sat down in a chair beside Sheila's desk so I could look at the former detective's face. He seemed embarrassed.

"The thing is, I still believe it was carefully planned, but...," and Mr. Boruvka ran his index finger around the inside of his collar; even in this heat he was wearing a threadbare tweed jacket and the kind of tie that's always referred to as conservative. "Unluckily I forgot to consider one circumstance, and that is— well, there is no excuse and I apologize, Miss Sullivan."

"That's all right," Sheila replied in her businesslike tone. "What circumstance?"

"Not long ago, Mrs. McCavish interviewed me for her newspaper, *Torontska Dama.* You have heard of it?"

Sheila nodded and looked at me. In fact, she'd read excerpts from the interview that Jirina had sold to the *Toronto Sun.*

"We talked mostly about prison conditions in Czechoslovakia," Mr. Boruvka went on, "but when I left Mrs. McCavish told me that one night some days before, a man with a stocking over his face had attacked her and stolen her purse. This was in Etobicoke, yes? The man ran around a corner and Mrs. McCavish heard a car engine suddenly roar. Do you see? The driver didn't start the motor; it was going already and he just put it to the gear and drove off. Mrs. McCavish called the police from a phone booth, and they found her handbag around the corner, where the thieves threw it away."

"She was mugged?" Sheila looked surprised. "Why didn't she tell us about it yesterday?"

"She doesn't like to talk about such things—if you'll pardon me for saying it—to Canadians."

"What is there to be ashamed of? Muggings are pretty common here these days. Another gift from our Big Brother to the south. Was she carrying a lot of money or valuables?"

"She had credit cards and twenty dollars or so," said the former detective awkwardly. "That is what makes no sense to me. I think the man wanted something else. Perhaps they took the money just to hide that. Because there was a document someone smuggled out of Prague and gave to her, and that was stolen too—"

"Do you mean to say, Mr. Boruvka," Sheila interrupted in a tone I had hoped she'd abandoned, "that someone from Prague was following Mrs. McCavish around waiting for the chance to waylay her, just to get his hands on some cheap gossip?"

"Yes, but it was a *typewritten* document," said Boruvka diffidently. "As you know, typewriters can be traced more easily than handwriting. The police in Prague have samples of type from all the typewriters sold in the shops, so once they possess a document, it's not hard to find the machine it was written on."

"You mean they go to all that trouble just because some politician slept with a ballet dancer?"

"What they want to know is who spreads the documents around and who smuggles them out," said the detective, running his finger around the inside of his collar again. "What the documents say is not so important. They must have found out that one of the people who gives Mrs. McCavish information lives in Etobicoke, and they were following her—"

"Who are 'they'?"

That flexible pronoun turned out to have yet another meaning.

"I mean resident agents."

"You too! Why does everyone seem to think Toronto is crawling with Czech spies?"

"Crawling?" Boruvka looked mystified.

"Full of spies," I explained.

"*Full* is maybe not the right word," he said uneasily. "And they are not spies like Mr. Kim Philby. But they exist."

"And they're following Mrs. McCavish around?"

"Yes, I'm afraid they are," said Mr. Boruvka, reddening. "Think about it. Etobicoke is not a poor part of town. Is it plausible that a mugging—"

"Last month alone," said Sheila, "Toronto had about a hundred incidents like it. Women are just not safe on the streets any more. Of course, it's nothing compared to New York, but we're moving in that direction. Have you ever been to New York, Mr. Boruvka?"

The former detective shook his head. "Zuzanka took me to see Niagara Falls once."

"That's too bad. I've been to New York. And I've also been to Havana." I looked at Sheila. Several years earlier, she had spent thirteen days of a two-week excursion to Cuba sunbathing on a beach exclusively reserved for Westerners who sympathized with the revolution. "I don't want to comment on the political system there because I know it's not perfect," she went on, "but one thing is undeniable—the crime rate has been radically reduced. Even in a large city like Havana, there's law and order."

The former detective nodded eagerly. "Order, yes, of course," he said, "but I'm not so certain of the crime rate. When I was still working in Prague—"

"Incidentally, what were you actually in prison for, Mr. Boruvka?" Sheila interrupted him again. "Your daughter says it was for political reasons."

"Yes," said Boruvka. "That's basically correct."

"Basically?"

He told us the story. When the Soviet Union had invaded Czechoslovakia in 1968, a family now living in Pittsburgh had escaped, leaving their six-year-old daughter behind with the grandmother. When all their efforts to get their child released to join them in the West failed, they arranged to have a gangster with the improbable name of Joe Bomb (obviously an alias) spirit their child out of Czechoslovakia in a light airplane. The plane was piloted by a friend of the detective's daughter who used the "kidnapping"—as it was called in the Czech press— to escape himself. He's now a pilot with American Airlines. Boruvka's role in the plot was to cover the getaway, and to do so he had to hold his fellow policemen at gunpoint while the plane took off. There was no room for Boruvka in the plane, and he was nailed. He claimed he knew all along they'd get him, but I think he must have hoped he could shoot his way out. His explanation for getting involved in the scheme was too thin. "I'd had enough," he said, but he wouldn't be any more precise than that. Unfortunately, during the escape the gangster Joe Bomb had shot and killed an important Communist official. Boruvka ended up getting fifteen years as an accessory. He got off so lightly, he said, because they took his former services into consideration. He refused to explain how he had escaped from prison.

I observed Sheila's dilemma. The rescue of a child held captive by a police state won her sympathy, but a family that had chosen to emigrate to the United States was less appealing. And decent people simply do not accept help from Yankees. On the other hand, Joe Bomb wasn't a member of a criminal organization like the CIA or the FBI, but a common gangster—which meant, in her ideology, that he was a victim of the system. This was a plus. Of course, the murder of an important Communist official smelled of General Pinochet. But on the other side of the argument was Boruvka's evident heroism and the fact that he himself had been a prisoner. Sheila was hopelessly caught in a tangle of conflicting sympathies and antipathies.

"At first Mrs. McCavish thought Prague would not worry about what she did," Boruvka went on. "She did not take care. She left things lying around and she would be away for many days with no one at home to look after the house. One time she left the whole subscription list for *Torontska Dama* on the kitchen table and someone broke in and took photographs of it."

"How did she find out?"

"The people who subscribe to her magazine started to get printed notices that *Torontska Dama* was bankrupt, out of business because of financial problems. But the trick did not work because readers began to send cheques to support the magazine—Mrs. McCavish didn't really need the money, but that was how she found out what had happened. So she published a denial—"

"Didn't they know Mrs. McCavish was well off?"

"It wasn't a very smart plan," agreed Boruvka. "Some of the things they do, you can never make much sense out of them, and besides, that plan actually helped Mrs. McCavish out, in a political sense. There were many old émigrés who suspected that she was a Communist in disguise. Because she had been allowed to work at Expo '67 in Montreal. Then this happened and everybody could see that the police in Prague were trying to discredit her, so the émigrés began to trust her."

The detective's daughter stepped into the room and announced that Vogeltanz would not be coming because his secretary had forgotten to give him the message. She was just going to leave again when Sheila asked her to stay to hear her father's new hypothesis about Heather's murder. Sue turned to her father with a look of unfalsified admiration. She didn't behave at all like a proper watchful sister.

"It's like this," said her father. "At first I thought we must try to find out who knew that Mrs. McCavish wouldn't be home. I forgot—perhaps because I have not had so much practice for a few years—about that mugging incident. But now I think we should try to find out who *didn't* know she wouldn't be home. Because you see," and Boruvka finally loosened his tie and unbuttoned his collar, "I think Miss Donby was killed by mistake. Mrs. McCavish was the one they were after."

Sheila leaned back in her chair and for a moment she ceased to look like the intelligent woman she usually was. Sue was gazing at her father with something like worship in her eyes. Personally, I was wondering whether the detective was suffering from a hyperactive imagination or whether it was we who were short in that department.

Sheila was the first to come to her senses. "That can't be right," she said, in a tone that was close to exasperation. "The murderer would have to be blind. How else could he make a mistake like that?"

The former detective was clearly uncomfortable, but it wasn't his hypothesis that was troubling him. "Blind?" he asked, in a slightly befuddled manner. "No, he was not blind. But you know, Miss Sullivan, if you'll excuse me, there is another possibility. Perhaps the murderer didn't know his victim."

Sheila blushed right down to her décolletage. "So you think the murder was committed during an attempted burglary?"

"That would be—well, logically that might be possible too," admitted the detective, but before he could continue Sheila had regained her usual confidence.

"But armed burglars," she said, putting a cigarette into her mouth with an elegant motion, "very seldom get rattled enough to bungle a job like that."

"I wasn't thinking of a burglar. I meant a hired murderer. Hired murderers do not steal."

Sheila's cigarette fell into her lap. The detective went on, awkwardly. "Most of the time, a hired murderer doesn't know his victim. He is only told where the victim will be at a certain time. If the victim is expected to be alone, a general description is enough."

The cigarette burned through Sheila's dress and brought her to her feet. She picked it up, masterfully concealed her embarrassment, and went on the offensive. "Are you seriously trying to tell me that here in Toronto, where we have one of the finest homicide squads in the world, the Czech government would actually risk murdering a woman? And a Canadian citizen, at that?"

Boruvka ran his handkerchief under his unbuttoned collar. "That is why they would hire someone, no? Since there is not a personal relationship between the killer and his victim, all deductions on the basis of *cui bono*—who benefits—are harder to make. Besides that, hired murderers have, well, what you could call a professional code of ethics. They never reveal who hired them, not even in countries where they still have the death penalty. If they did, their, uh, colleagues would physically liquidate them because otherwise the trade would lose its credibility and they would be out of work."

"But Mr. Boruvka," said Sheila, almost losing her temper, "you can't expect us to believe that the Czech government would commit murder just to prevent the publication of gossip and rumour? Because no matter how you look at it, that's all *Toronto Lady* is."

Boruvka wiped the perspiration from the back of his neck. "The thing is, Miss Sullivan, I am not suggesting they wanted to kill Mrs. McCavish because of her newspaper. I only doubt the hypothesis as it is now. I only wanted to say that the motive may not have been jealousy or some other, uh, reason of the heart. Of course," he added apologetically, "you did not know about the mugging, so you could not—"

"So what do you think the motive was, then?"

"I—I do not know," replied the former detective nervously. "But I would guess that politics is mixed up in it somehow. At least," he added sadly, "as far as we Czechs are concerned, politics is mixed up in everything."

Upon hearing the word "politics" Sheila regained her poise, for in anything to do with that subject, she felt on solid ground. The ideologies she had absorbed left no room for doubt. Looking like Jane Fonda mounting the barricades, she was about to reply, when Boruvka got out of his chair, excused himself again, and left for his afternoon shift. Sheila saw him to the door, thanked him for his suggestions, and then came back and plopped down into her chair.

"What do you think, Neil?" she asked. "It's an interesting hypothesis, but it's all so circumstantial and far-fetched. He's really just going on unconfirmed feelings, and frankly, like a lot of immigrants, he still seems to be living in Central Europe. I don't think he's quite used to the way things are done here. I mean, can you honestly believe a foreign government would resort to murder just to suppress a harmless scandal sheet?"

She walked over to her desk and pulled out a bottle of Black Velvet.

I was unsure where Boruvka's theory left my own hypothesis but I was anxious for Sheila to know what I'd found out, so while she was pouring generous drinks for both of us, I told her about my sister's midnight call to the Savoy Hotel and about Count Trcka and his mysterious heraldic society. As far as I was concerned, Trcka had a racket going, and that in itself put him outside the law. What the racket had to do with my sister, if anything, I wasn't sure, but I was determined to find out.

Perhaps Trcka had discovered her propensity for titled men and had offered to check a few pedigrees, for a price.

Sheila listened silently to what I had to say while she twirled her drink slowly, the ice cubes clinking against the glass. I wondered, did Marlowe take his with ice? At twenty-five dollars a day plus expenses?

"Let's get them together," Sheila said finally.

"Who?" I asked.

"Count what's-his-name and Jirina McCavish. If he was the one who killed Heather, we might get an interesting reaction out of him when he's confronted with the woman who owns the house where it took place. And if he was a hired killer and made a mistake.... But I can't bring myself to believe that. I'm sorry, Neil, but I still think there's more emotion than political intrigue in this case. You know how macho those Eastern European men are."

I thought about the diffident detective who had just left the office. He certainly didn't fit that mould, although I had to admit that Herman Chumac did.

"And I can't believe she doesn't know the count, either," Sheila went on. "How can the editor of a gossip sheet not know a prominent member of her own community? It doesn't make sense."

"It's not the only thing about this case that doesn't make sense," I said.

6

Confrontation

When I phoned the Savoy Hotel to persuade the count to come to our little meeting, a voice with an unmistakable West Indian accent told me that Mr. Trcka was in Toronto on business and that he could most probably be found at the Old English Pub.

Another business trip? For a hotel manager, the count seemed to spend a good deal of his time on the road. And at the Old English Pub, although Herman, the pub manager, claimed he didn't know Trcka personally. At least, he hadn't yesterday.

Count Trcka was at the restaurant as predicted. When I told him my name over the phone, there was a long pause and then, somewhat reluctantly, he said, "What can I do for you?"

I said I had to talk to him about a matter of mutual concern. What would that be, he asked. I replied that I'd rather tell him when we met. His reaction was not what you'd expect of a hotel manager: "Look here," he said, rather shrilly, "I'm an extremely busy man. I can't waste my time with someone I don't know, talking about something you won't explain."

"I don't think you can afford not to meet me," I said. There was another pause, but he didn't hang up. I said nothing for a moment, to give his nerves the proper edge, and then continued:

"I can give you a hint. It concerns a lady in whose house something happened, putting her in a rather unpleasant and delicate situation; it appears you might be able to help her. The lady in question thinks you know something that might support a claim she is making."

"Who is she?" he asked after a pause. My name and the hint were obviously making him think.

"I'm sorry, I can't tell you that yet. The lady asked me not to reveal her identity. But she knows you by reputation and says she's depending on you to be"—and I paused—"a gentleman."

He said nothing.

"I'll tell you one more thing," I said, after another well-timed pause. "The lady is a compatriot of yours."

That was a good move. How could a gentleman refuse to come to the aid of a lady in distress, especially if they shared a homeland?

Besides, Trcka knew who I was—and he had to assume that I'd found out about his relationship with my sister. He could see that if he didn't come to me, I'd go to him.

He sighed heavily and accepted. Did his voice tremble as he spoke? Perhaps. He had good reason to be nervous—if he was the one who'd pulled the trigger that night, and ended my sister's life.

Sheila didn't have to explain to Jirina what she wanted to talk to her about. The editor was always willing to talk to anybody about anything.

Next morning, Sheila and I were sitting at a sidewalk café in Yorkville called The French Crêperie, waiting with growing suspense. I had deliberately invited the count a half-hour later than Jirina because I was familiar enough by now with her Central European sense of time.

The count arrived with the punctuality of a good businessman, and he was dressed like one, too, in a light grey three-piece suit and a yellow tie held in place with a garnet tie-pin.

I stood up and introduced myself. The man was much less genial than his picture. Those steely grey eyes above his prominent, aristocratic nose looked straight at me. They were cold and humourless and in spite of myself I felt the back of my neck tingle. Then, with all the formal politeness I could muster, I introduced him to Sheila.

Before we could sit down, Jirina McCavish hurried up. She was exactly thirty minutes late.

"Thirty minutes late, on the dot!" I greeted the editor, who was a little out of breath. "I'd like you to meet Mr. Trcka. Mr. Trcka—Mrs. McCavish," I said, looking from one to the other to see any signs of surprise—or the lack of it.

"So you're Trcka!" exclaimed Jirina enthusiastically. "Say, I've heard a lot of interesting rumours about you and your heraldic society. How would you like to be interviewed for my newspaper?"

Trcka stared at Jirina as though caught completely off balance; even I was surprised at her directness. He said, "Why, of course, if you think...," and his voice trailed off, though he continued to stare at her as if he were unsure she was really there. I'd seen that glassy-eyed stare before. Trcka wasn't the first man to lose himself in the mist of the editor's blue-grey eyes. I had been present when Tim McCavish first succumbed. On the other hand, if there had been a mistake in identity—and if he was the one who'd made it—he was now confronting....

There was a pause. Sheila, who was extremely nervous about the situation, began making small talk about the weather. This gave me a chance to study Trcka. His brow was furrowed. He must have been wondering just what was behind this apparently innocent meeting.

When our crêpes had arrived, and the conversation about the food and the unrelenting heat wave began to flag, I barged in with a question I hoped would produce some interesting reactions, at least interesting enough to let us draw some conclusions. "Jirina," I asked, keeping one eye on Trcka, "why exactly did you invite Vogeltanz to have supper with you on the night my sister was murdered?"

It was a bolt out of the blue, and Trcka looked at me sharply for the first time since we'd sat down, but Jirina was entirely unruffled.

"There's nothing secret about it," she replied willingly. "Vogeltanz travels to Austria a lot on business and it's only a couple of hours by train from Vienna to Prague. Anyway, he offered to undertake some—well, let's just call them transactions—for me in Prague."

I was already familiar with the way she would stop herself at crucial moments in her conversation. She loved to talk, but she felt she had to protect her sources, so she had developed a conversational style that was full of innuendo and deliberate mystification, not unlike the way some of my business acquaintances talked about impending deals. She looked at the count and, as though aware for the first time of the intensity of his gaze, she stammered briefly before regaining her usual fluency.

"Do you really want me to go into this?"

"I think you should," I replied.

"Well, the thing is that Vogeltanz is Austrian himself and during the war he served in the German army. He thinks he knows something about a man who, well, to put it simply, who was responsible for the death of my poor father." She stopped and took a large mouthful of crêpes.

Sheila was gasping. "The Fascists killed your father?"

"The Nazis," Mrs. McCavish corrected her with a full mouth. "I was a baby when it happened, back in 1942. He was beaten to death at Gestapo headquarters in Prague. The chief interrogator was a terrible sadist. He had a sign over his desk in German that read, 'Anyone who laughs in here has a real sense of humour.' My father didn't talk."

Tears welled in Sheila's eyes. It was a reflex reaction whenever the subject of killing came up, at least in connection with Americans or Fascists.

"And you know who it was?" she whispered.

"I know who put the finger on him. A real bastard, a Czech collaborator—at least, I think he was Czech. Anyway, a Gestapo agent. And I have proof. That is—" and once again she stopped. "I think I can identify him. No one knows this, but my mother managed—" and she stopped a third time. This time she didn't try to pick up the thread. "And I know what he looks like," she went on. "His nickname was Freddy the Nose. His real name— or at least the name he went by then—was Ferdinand Burda, but they called him the Nose because he had a gigantic hooked nose, like Mr. Punch. Mother said it was enormous and unforgettable."

We all looked at Trcka. Suddenly, his aristocratic nose seemed enormous and unforgettable.

Trcka noticed our glances but displayed no sign of discomfort or self-consciousness. He went back to staring at the editor.

Jirina obviously had no intention of telling us any more. Suddenly she looked at her watch, gasped, and mumbled something about having a very important meeting. She asked the count for his business card and said she'd call him about the interview. Then she got out of her chair. The count was on his feet in a flash, gallantly held her chair for her, and said he had to go as well. Before Sheila or I really knew what was happening, he had said goodbye and guided Jirina, who threw a questioning glance over her shoulder at us, out into the street.

When they were gone, Sheila collected her wits and stood up too. "I think I'd better keep an eye on them, just in case."

"But they'll be speaking Czech," I objected.

"It doesn't matter," Sheila replied. "Wait for me back at the office."

And Sheila the shamusess blended expertly into the Yorkville noon-hour crowds, leaving me with four plates of unfinished crêpes and a host of unanswered questions. Belatedly, the waitress arrived with a large carafe of the house wine, described on the menu as French. It must have been genuine, because it was expensive and miserable.

"Has Vogeltanz called yet?" I asked Sue when I got back to Sheila's office.

"Good Lord, I forgot about him!" cried Sue, dismayed. "I'll call him at once."

I watched her silently as she punched out the numbers, waited, and then asked to speak to Mr. von Vogeltanz. A long murmuring in the receiver followed. Sue interjected several times with an "Oh no!" and once with an "Oh my God!" and finally said, "All right, I promise not to tell him. But please, next time tie a knot on your—on whatever you want, okay?"

Sue hung up and said, "Either Vogeltanz's secretary is pregnant, or she's in love. She's forgotten to give him the message again, and it's the third time she's done it. She begged me not to tell her boss because she's afraid he'll fire her."

"All right," I sighed. "Try reaching him again tomorrow if he doesn't call back today. Try him every hour. It's urgent."

I went into Sheila's office, sat down at her desk, and opened the drawer. Although she had an elegant liquor cabinet in the office, the bottle was in the right place. I pulled out the rye and a glass. I found it odd that Philip Marlowe was Sheila's favourite fictional detective—not only because she seemed to believe that most literature from Chaucer onwards was a male conspiracy, but also because I'd always seen Marlowe—thanks to Bogart, perhaps—as a guy whose manners with women were somewhat unpolished. Sheila disabused me of these post-feminist delusions by letting me know that Marlowe was really very respectful of women; quite a few characters, such as Adrienne Fromsett in *The Lady in the Lake*, demonstrate his respect. It seems she gained this view from a course on popular American fiction given by some Czech professor of American Lit. Another conman, from the sound of it. Besides, Sheila added, Marlowe was a socialist at heart because he longed for a more just society. This was probably her own observation; I doubt that any Czech professor would praise Marlowe for that. And as for Miss Adrienne Fromsett—didn't she succumb to the charms of a man Marlowe described as a "nice piece of beef"? Not quite the thing for a strong, self-respecting woman to do.

I poured myself a glass of rye and took a long, slow sip. Suddenly there was a click in my brain. The forgetful secretary—what if she'd forgotten to pass on Jirina's message to her boss that day? That dinner was off because the editor had to go out on important business? Vogeltanz would have arrived at Sackville Street....

But Vogeltanz knew Jirina.

Another click. The former detective had mentioned the possibility of a professional killer.

Trcka? Hardly a man who needed to make extra money as a hired gun. But his behaviour today *was* suspicious. Or maybe it was just that old black magic, as it had been with Tim McCavish. As for Trcka's nose, the idea was preposterous. There must be a thousand noses like it around. It was hardly positive identification. And how old was Trcka, anyway? If he was about fifty now, then he couldn't have been more than eighteen at the time Jirina's father was led away to his death.

And in any case, what could this legendary Freddy the Nose possibly have to do with my sister's death?

It was the first time I had asked myself that question. It would not be the last.

The door opened. Sheila walked in and slowly sat down in the chair normally reserved for clients. I poured her a double Marlowe and slid the glass across the desk towards her.

"Well?"

"They went to a bar together," Sheila said, taking a sip. "The count seemed very upset and as the conversation went on he got more and more agitated, until finally he got up, paid the bill, and left in a taxi. Jirina left too. I expect she went on to that appointment, if she really had one." Sheila stopped, took a drink, then continued. "Neil, something funny's going on here. What do you make of it?"

"I'm not sure," I said. I felt the desk-drawer whisky doing its work. Despite the errors in judgement and tactics I'd made in the past two days, I was beginning to feel like a real, hard-boiled detective. "Maybe we're on a wild goose chase, but we'll never know until we follow it through."

Sheila was silent. Suddenly, I felt like a cigar. Whisky sometimes does that to me. I took out my silver case, took out a cigar, and lit up. The taste was disgusting and I snatched it out of my mouth and looked at it. It wasn't my usual brand. Then I looked at the case.

The initials H.C. were engraved on one corner.

So that was it. Back in the Old English Pub, I had inadvertently picked up the cigar case belonging to the man who might be responsible for my kid sister's death.

7

A Hot Night

There was nothing more we could do that day, so I went home early to get some sleep. The temperature was in the nineties, even after dark, and the city was steaming like a coin laundry on a Sunday morning. The air, thick with that enervating humidity, stuck to the skin like perspiration, and even a cold shower provided no more than temporary relief. The air conditioner in my room was broken. This was the month of heart attacks, Legionnaires' disease, anxiety, and apocalyptic foreboding. I spent the night in damp sheets in horizontal motion around a vertical axis.

It was all psychological, the morbid effect of an excess of BTUs in the atmosphere. But I couldn't shake the premonition of imminent danger, of a catastrophe hanging in the air, waiting to befall us. The reddish, perspiring moon glowed through the open window in the stifling darkness, and my sister came back to my thoughts, as she often had in the last few days. That obscure victim of rebellion against convention—gone, vanished from the world in the tritest of all ways: a crime of passion. Or was it?

In the suffocating heat I was no longer certain of anything. Could the former detective be right? Had my sister's death been not the natural result of her lifestyle, but some obscene intrusion from a world unknown to us? Was it possible that this confused little girl had been struck down by powers on a distant battlefield, powers I'd never really believed existed outside the pages of spy novels?

About five o'clock I gave up and took another shower. My eye was caught by a red glimmer outside; my father was sitting on the second-floor deck, smoking a cigar in the darkness. Congealed strands of smoke, like heavy serpents, curled lazily over the wooden rail and disappeared down into the garden below. I felt sorry for my father. I slid open the glass door leading to the deck and walked over to him. He quickly rubbed his eyes, but when he turned his face to me his cheeks were glistening, and it wasn't sweat.

"Hot," I said.

Dad nodded.

"Has your—" I wanted to ask him if his air conditioner had broken down too, just to make conversation, but I stopped. I knew why he was sitting here in the humid night instead of sleeping. When my mother died ten years ago, he used to sit like this at night and smoke his coronary-inducing but comforting cigars.

I sank back into a wicker chair and lit one myself, taking it from a box that lay on the round table beside my father's chair.

"I've found something out," he said. "Tomorrow I'm going to call the police about it, even though—"

"What is it?"

"I had a—well, a hunch. I phoned Bell Telephone and—Heather...." His voice broke and he quickly inhaled a mouthful of smoke and veiled himself in a grey-white mask. "Someone called Kitchener that day—the day she was.... You were out the whole day. It could only have been...," and tears crept into his voice again, "...only our poor little girl."

"What number did she call?"

"It was a hotel."

"Which one?"

"The Savoy," said my father wearily. "I have no idea whether it's even important, but I'm reporting it to the police just in case it has a bearing."

The count again? But how could Heather have known then that she'd be alone at Jirina's that evening? She wouldn't have known that until later in the day, when she arrived, let herself in with her key, and found Jirina's note to Mrs. Etherington.

Something hummed lazily around me, then tiny legs tickled my wrist. I raised my right hand to kill the miniature vampire, but I stopped. Ah, Lord, an absurd inhibition. The house was still heavy with my sister's death and the August heat penetrated it like a poisonous vapour, an omen. I let my right hand fall back onto the armrest and the little creature pierced my skin and drank my blood. It was irritating, but I did nothing about it. After a time, I blew it away with a jet of smoke. It lurched heavily into the air, and its monstrous, leggy shadow hovered unsteadily against the red canopy of sky above the maples.

"Neil," said my father, "it's partly my fault too. I had a terrible argument with her the day before. That's why she went off to her girlfriend's—"

"Don't blame yourself, Dad," I said reassuringly. "I had an argument with her every day, and she spent the night with her girlfriends at least a hundred times."

It was usually with her boyfriends, but I didn't say that to him.

"But she always came back. This time—"

An absurd conclusion to one life. What kind of life had it been? Too short to admit any conclusions. She was in diapers until she was almost four; the parents were reluctant to force her to sit on the potty because a radical pediatrician claimed it could cause irreparable psychological damage. They were terribly kind and terribly indulgent, and they wanted only the best for us, but they were afraid to punish us, afraid to offer us firm guidance, afraid to stand up to our whims. Later in life, when I looked through those child-rearing books they were always consulting, they seemed pointless. But my parents wanted to keep up with the times. They had a horror of being thought backward. My father, old now and a retired businessman, had even voted NDP in the last election.

Then, when my sister was eleven, my mother died.

It wasn't until long after her death that my father finally stopped reading those do-it-yourself child psychology books. His nerves finally gave out. But even then, he never laid a hand on my sister in anger. Instead, he began to argue with her, plead with her. But it was too late. My uninhibited sister was beyond the point of recall.

And nobody ever hit her. She didn't receive that kind of treatment from any man until she met Herman Chumac. Maybe he sensed a lack in her upbringing and tried to compensate for it, in his crude, Middle European way. But that final blow—a piece of lead in her heart—who delivered that? And why?

A few hours before she was killed she telephoned someone in Kitchener.

Perhaps my father knew more about these things than I did. He loved Heather. I was only fond of her.

"Who did she know in Kitchener?" I asked.

The old man, my liberal and progressive father, slowly shook his head. "I didn't know her friends. I deliberately refrained from taking any interest in them. There were so many of them, so many—" At moments like these, his voice did not serve him well.

"You don't happen to have the number she called, do you?"

He reached into his pocket, took out a piece of paper, and handed it to me. I went inside and checked the file of telephone bills. The number was the same one she had called a couple of weeks ago. What had she said to him this time? What had he said to her?

I wondered if I shouldn't report everything I'd learned today to Bill Kendrick. According to the law, I should. And even common sense told me that the chances of our unravelling the deepening mystery ourselves were small. Yet in crucial moments, reason seldom dominates. Every time I thought of Heather's murder, I felt a new surge of hatred, so strong it overwhelmed me. Such extremes of human emotions were new to me. I had had minor affairs with several women but in all honesty I don't think I had ever experienced genuine passion. Even in my relationship with Sheila, that "red consuming flame" that's supposed to burn up a man's reason was dampened by what popular magazines call a fear of being inadequate in bed. I had had minor altercations with my friends, but my dislike of losing my self-control had always held me back, and I had never felt moved by genuine hatred. But now the sensation swept over me like an invasion from some strange, foreign world.

And then the former detective and his daughter were always coming up in my thoughts, God knows why. What was the mystery of their impenetrable sadness, never quite banished by their daily struggle to earn a living here? Did they have some sensitivity to the tragic dimensions of life that we over here had lost? Yet the Donbys once lived in Europe too, and they risked the stormy Atlantic in small wooden ships to escape the persecutions that came from rigid religious ideologies. Perhaps the mystery of those reactionary Middle Europeans is no mystery at all, but something that's become submerged in us over the generations. Perhaps the larger sense of life is there in all of us, waiting only for larger events to release it. Events like murder, like some bastard—

But the Donbys do not capitulate before the bastards of this world. I decided that, unlike my father, I would be conservative and traditional. And that I would make room in my spirit for those larger, more ancient emotions that were now clamouring for recognition.

8

A Tale from a Far Country

Sheila called me at nine the next morning to say that she had
finally got hold of Vogeltanz, and that he had agreed to meet us at
her office. An hour later, with rather disconcerting promptness,
there he was, sitting in Sheila's waiting room drinking Coca Cola
from a glass taken from Sheila's secret drawer. He had refused
the proffered whisky, saying he never drank before lunch.

Vogeltanz was the second aristocrat to enter the story. This
one, perhaps, was authentic. When Sheila showed him a snapshot
of my sister, he even pulled out a monocle and squinted at the
picture carefully. Yes, he announced, it was the same one the
police had shown him. But regrettably, he went on, he had known
her only superficially. He recalled seeing her once at a party, but
he couldn't remember much about her, and what little he did
know didn't help to explain why anyone would have wanted her
dead. He stared at the snapshot a while longer, then removed his
monocle, expressed his condolences in a very proper manner,
and lit a cigarette in a silver holder.

Vogeltanz had practically no accent when he spoke English,
but he laced his conversation generously with German words
that sounded genuine. He was willing, he said, to do anything

within his power to help us track down the killer. After all, that was why he had agreed to come, although he had already told everything he knew, which admittedly wasn't much, to the relevant authorities. "Relevant authorities" were the words he used. It sounded like a translation to me.

"We invited you here because of something that doesn't appear to relate directly to the case," said Sheila. "I'm sure you can understand that we have to investigate *all* the circumstances."

He nodded. "Of course. The whole affair must be very distressing to both of you."

"We've learned," Sheila went on, "that Mrs. McCavish invited you to have supper with her at her house the night of the murder, and that she called it off at the last minute. Did she have any particular reason for inviting you there in the first place?" Sheila was trying to find out if Vogeltanz would give us the same story Jirina had.

"Of course, I understand what you're getting at," replied Vogeltanz. "There are things that are not always easy to explain to *den Nichteuropäern*—to non-Europeans. Have you heard of the term *samizdat*?"

Sheila had encountered this expression in her period of fascination with the victims of Marxism. I had first heard the expression from her, and Jirina once told me that it referred to a kind of underground literature that was circulated by hand in socialist countries.

"As you know," Vogeltanz continued, "*Frau* McCavish is constantly on the lookout for new material for her magazine. But it is hard to get it out of Czechoslovakia, for you have to smuggle it out and the Czech *Grenzpolizei* are like ferrets where *samizdat* are concerned. Anything written," he said, with a smile, "interests them more than drugs or contraband jewellery. This is where I come in. Since I do regular business with the Czechs, they tend to be less thorough, shall we say, in checking my luggage."

He drew on his pale blue cigarette and a conspicuous furrow appeared on his cheek, reaching right to his nose. I had seen such scars once before, during a visit to *Oktoberfest* in Munich, and Hilde—who otherwise has nothing to do with this story, except that she taught me more German in two weeks than I'd managed to learn from Professor Heidenreich at the university (true, I dropped his course after ten weeks)—explained that they were duelling scars, for duelling with swords was an illegal but honoured custom in German universities right up to the arrival of the man who finally diverted all that Teutonic flirtation with absolutes and death into more up-to-date and socially useful channels. Could Vogeltanz have been a student that long ago? If he was, he must not have earned any kind of academic title, or he'd be flaunting it now in the manner of so many Central Europeans.

"Perhaps it would be more accurate to say," the man went on, "that I *intended* to come into the picture. I had offered my services to Mrs. McCavish and that evening we were to have met and worked out the details. Unfortunately...," and he spread his hands in a gesture of mute sympathy.

This was more or less what the owner of *Toronto Lady* had begun to tell us before suddenly changing the subject. So to try to trip him up, I said, "But Mrs. McCavish told us something entirely different."

The aristocrat turned his eyes on me for the first time. They were round, blue, almost good-natured. They didn't suit him at all. There was something in them that reminded me of the former detective. He carefully tapped the ash off his cigarette and replied, "Ah, then Mrs. McCavish must have told you *die andere Geschichte*—the other story."

"You mean—?"

"About the man with the large nose," said Mr. von Vogeltanz, sipping his Coke. He held his little finger with its signet ring erect, as though he were drinking mocha from a cup of Meissen china. His intent blue eyes studied the silent rapport between Sheila and me.

"What do you know about it?" asked Sheila.

Mr. von Vogeltanz crossed his legs. He was wearing an expensive, and probably illegal, pair of snakeskin shoes. "No more than what *Frau* McCavish told me. His nose was said to be remarkably large, something like that actor—what was his name?"

"Jimmy Durante?" I proffered.

"*Genau*," laughed Mr. von Vogeltanz. "I don't think it's any secret that my interest in *Frau* McCavish is not entirely confined to—*wie soll ich es sagen*—to business, nor was my offer of help entirely without ulterior motives. In any case, I'm a businessman. I could hardly pretend that I was helping her, at considerable personal risk, merely because I sympathized with her politics." He slipped another cigarette into his holder. It looked like an expensive antique. "Politically, I am neutral. I import racing bobsleds and other products from the Eastern zone—for which some of my more political friends rather sharply criticize me— but I keep my money in Western banks, for which they do not. Thus, as I've already said, I travel rather more freely back and forth than the average tourist."

He stopped, lifted his glass of Coke, and continued. "Therefore I have also given a great deal of thought to the problem of this man with the very large nose. As *Frau* McCavish must have told you, he is responsible for *den Heldentod*—the heroic death—of her father."

And he raised his glass, as if in a toast to the memory of Jirina's poor dead father.

"*Und aus den Kriegserinnerungen...*," he said, and seemed to fall into a reverie. "War," he began again, "brands itself into one's memory as nothing else does. Years afterward, I can still recall details, scenes, even nuances of the weather and atmosphere, as if they happened only yesterday. Sometimes more vividly, in fact. I fought on the Eastern Front in my time." Vogeltanz noticed that this remark had made Sheila sit up and he laughed. It was a dignified laugh. "I'm afraid I was neither very courageous nor very eager as a soldier," he said. "We Austrians became warriors on the side of the Third Reich not of our own will, but by historical accident, as it were."

"I know," Sheila said. "The Anslus."

"*Anschluss*, madame, if I may be so bold as to amend your charming pronunciation. Ah, but I had no intention of indulging in sentimental wartime memories," he laughed. "As I was pondering the sad case of *Frau* McCavish's father, I was reminded of a certain unforgettable incident that took place in the Ukraine near a village that became generally famous after the war. It was called ——"

The name meant nothing to either Sheila or myself, and when Mr. von Vogeltanz had determined this with his eyes, he went on to explain. "The SS slaughtered several thousand Jews there." Once more he noticed Sheila's reaction, and laughed again. "Don't worry, madame, I was not with the SS, but rather with the Second Alpine Hunters' Division of *das Heer Ostmark. Ostmark* was how the Nazis referred to Austria."

Sheila was visibly relieved. In any case, the gentleman with the monocle didn't look like an SS man. But then, neither of us had ever seen an SS man, except in the movies.

"We didn't know, of course, what had happened in the village," Vogeltanz continued, "but something—*wie sagt man das*—something was in the air. The whole area had been cordoned off by a unit of the *Sicherheitspolizei* and a suspicious number of staff cars were prowling about. And also vehicles belonging to the *geheime Staatspolizei*."

He looked at Sheila.

"The—?" she queried.

"The Gestapo," he said. "I particularly remember those vehicles. One of them stopped in front of our headquarters. It was towards suppertime, and the commander of our unit invited the gentlemen in the staff car to dine with him. One of them was a civilian, or at least he wore civilian clothing. I saw him then, and I can still see him today. His expression was very—*ja, wie soll ich's ausdrücken*—unpleasant. Evil. Sinister."

"Why?" said Sheila, exhaling. I knew what he would say. But he said it in German.

"*Er hatte eine riesengrosse Adlernase.*"

A monumental nose.

He finished his Coca Cola and stroked his well-tended, grey-ing moustache with an equally well-manicured set of fingers.

"This is what I wanted to tell *Frau* McCavish that evening. And I wanted to offer her my help."

"What kind of help?" I asked, rather sharply.

He laughed. "I will not pretend that I had any really clear idea myself. This business of Nazi-hunting is certainly more difficult—and dangerous, even now—than the smuggling of a few manuscripts. And there are others more competent, and qualified, than myself. Nevertheless, I felt that if I were to contact my old comrades from the front, those who are still alive, they might perhaps remember something. In addition to his nose, this man cut quite an imposing figure. As he stood there against the background of the Ukrainian steppes, the sun was setting, and that nose of his—*kurz und gut*—such an *apparition*—it's the only word I can think of that suits—and we knew that something very…ugly…had taken place in that village."

"But there must be thousands of men with big noses. What makes you think he was the one responsible for Jirina's father's—"

"One of my friends was a junior officer who sat that night at the table with the Gestapo people. The man with the large nose was making jokes about the Czech resistance. It turned out he had recently been transferred from Prague. That narrows the field considerably, wouldn't you say?"

"How old do you think he was?" asked Sheila.

Vogeltanz thought for a while. "That, of course, is not easy to say. People age quickly in wartime. Or to put it more accurately, they tend to look older than they are." And he stroked his moustache and fell silent. How old was Vogeltanz? If *he* had aged during the war, he had certainly cultivated himself in the opposite direction afterward.

"Twenty-five? Thirty?" Vogeltanz said. "He looked as though he was approaching thirty. Of course, in our division we had eighteen-year-olds whose hair was turning grey. But as I've said, his physiognomy was unforgettable. I wondered—although it's probably out of the question—whether Mrs. McCavish might have a photograph. Perhaps the Czech police arrested him after the war; they might have a photograph in their files. Ah, but I doubt very much whether any of those files are accessible now."

He looked at Sheila with his blue eyes. They went well with his grey, made-to-measure suit. As if hypnotized, Sheila said, "She doesn't have a photograph. But—would you be willing to meet a man who also has a very large nose—just on the off chance?"

He looked at her thoughtfully, then at me. "Certainly. Any time. Of course it's been over thirty years. But I'd recognize a nose like that again, even among thousands of others."

He stood up to go.

"One more little detail," I said, rising with him. He looked at me affably. "What did you do after Mrs. McCavish called your supper engagement off?"

"I understand," he said. "I went to a restaurant for supper. I stayed there until almost midnight, because at the next table they were discussing a political question that I am particularly interested in, though, as I told you, politics in general leaves me indifferent. But this is a problem that my old homeland shares with *Frau* McCavish's. The gentlemen at the next table were Czechs. Unfortunately, I don't speak that language, much as I'd like to, but I was having supper with friends who do. They got embroiled in the discussion and because almost every Czech past a certain age can speak at least some German—another of those accidents of history—pretty soon we were all speaking my mother tongue. The argument was about whether it was a good idea for the Czechs to have established their own state back in 1918, or whether they ought to have remained within the framework of a democratized Austro-Hungarian federation."

I recalled a group of people I had seen in the Old English Pub swilling beer from an absurd glass boot. Mr. Vogeltanz, it seemed, had an alibi for that fateful evening.

9

Mrs. McCavish's Souvenir

The telephone buzzed. All that remained of von Vogeltanz's presence in the office was the faint aroma of musk. Sheila answered the phone, then motioned me to pick up the extension. We heard Jirina's voice, sounding more anxious than usual.

"Oh good, you're there. I've just discovered something and I don't know...."

Even her pause was odd. Jirina normally talked as though she were firing off a long burst from a machine gun.

"It was under a pile of junk on my desk. The police must have missed it."

"This is Neil here," I said. "What did you find?"

"A note from your sister. At least, I'm almost certain it's her handwriting."

My hand tightened on the receiver. "What does it say?"

"Just that she made a long-distance call from my phone. It's dated the same day she was...."

"To Kitchener?" I asked quietly.

"How did you know that?"

"The Savoy Hotel?"

"Christ!" said the owner of *Toronto Lady*. "How in hell did you know?" Suddenly her voice became alert. "Hey! It just occurs to me—why did you ask me to meet Trcka in the first place?"

I was about to acquaint her with Mr. Boruvka's theory that she rather than Heather had been the target for the allegedly hired gun, but then I didn't. It might have scared her out of her wits, and anyway it was just a hypothesis. I produced my own hypothesis, based on Heather's nocturnal call to Kitchener, and concocted a vaguely plausible rationale for the confrontation. To my relief, Jirina went for it.

"You may have something there! Come over to my place!"

We drove over to Sackville Street so fast that we narrowly escaped death as we rounded the corner of Carlton and Parliament.

"You may really have something there!" said the excited Jirina. "I couldn't get rid of him. He kept asking about Heather. Now it seems suspicious to me, since he'd sworn up and down that he didn't know her. But I didn't find it odd at the time because he was being so persistent. I was anxious to get back to work, and he wouldn't let me go."

"What did he want to know about her? Did he let anything slip that might have to do with those long-distance calls?"

Jirina shook her head. "I don't think so. But he looked as though his own sister had been done in—" She stopped. "I'm sorry, Neil, I didn't mean to—"

"It's all right," I said, trying to shake the image of my sister's face from my mind. It was cool in the room. Jirina's air conditioner was humming and we were drinking iced tea. But outside the house where my sister had died, the tropical heat was still oppressive.

"He looked like—well, like a nervous wreck. He started chain smoking and he was so upset that at one point he had two going at once. And he went on and on about Heather."

A cat miaowed somewhere, and Jirina furrowed her brow. "Stupid animal," she said irrelevantly, and got up. Outside the french doors in the kitchen a large tomcat was pacing solemnly up and down, rubbing its head on the glass, a dark silhouette against the sunlight. "I'll never be able to teach that creature to come into the house the same way he goes out. He'll only leave through the front door, and he'll only come back this way." She went to the kitchen and slid the panel back, and the cat slipped into the room and rubbed its head sensuously in her hand. "Call yourself intelligent?" said the owner of *Toronto Lady*, and pushed the french doors shut. A lock clicked and Jirina pulled at the handle to make sure the doors were secure. The animal followed her into the sitting room, lay down on the carpet right in front of the television set, directly in the stream of cool air flowing from the air conditioner, and curled up to go to sleep. It seemed like a perfectly intelligent thing to do.

The front door. The french doors. This cat had looked through those doors at Herman Chumac, and scratched at them imploringly with his pink paws—while behind the cat, obscured by the curtain, lay my dead sister.

So much for the locked-room mystery. The french doors locked automatically when they were shut. The hired gun—or the murderer, at any rate—had simply knocked at the front door. Heather had let him in and—afterwards—he'd locked the front door from inside by turning the knob, left through the french doors, and slid them shut.

That meant Heather knew him.

Or did it?

"It all seems very suspicious now," said the editor. "He also inquired about my father, and from the look on his face you'd have thought it was *his* father they'd beaten to death."

"What did you tell him?" I asked.

"Not much," she said, "because I don't know that much myself. I only know what Mother told me—" She suddenly stopped and caught herself. "Oh, what a goose I am! A playboy like that! My God! And just look at his nose! Of course, it's been over thirty years. I still carry them around with me all the time, but in fact I've stopped hoping I'll ever find Bignose. And now—" and she slapped her forehead so hard she almost fell backwards out of her chair. "I tell someone with a nose like that about it. What a jackass I am!"

"About what?"

"I told Trcka about the fingerprints."

It was another Czech yarn, but this one sounded authentic, perhaps because it happened so long ago. Contemporary myths always seem to me like fiction whereas I've always believed that the fabled Antigone really existed.

Jirina McCavish's mother must have been cut from the same cloth as those heroines of Greek mythology. That night, before her husband was led off to his death, the Gestapo turned their flat upside down looking for documents they never found and clearly did not need, for their intention all along had simply been to eliminate Jirina's father. During the search Bignose threw all the books out of the bookcase, but to get at them he had to slide back a glass panel that was meant to keep dust off the books. When the men in the leather coats had taken her husband away, Jirina's mother, instead of breaking down, walked coolly over to the bookcase, took out the glass panel, and wrapped it carefully in a sheet. Next morning she took it out of the house before she went to Gestapo headquarters to ask about her husband. They had an old family friend, a detective retired from the Prague Homicide Squad called Bohuslav Vodicka, and it was he who made certain that Bignose would not vanish without a trace.

To this day, the daughter of the murdered hero carried the fingerprints around with her in a plastic envelope, the kind people normally keep their driver's licences in.

When the owner of *Toronto Lady* realized the implications of having told all this to Trcka, she had a genuine, old-fashioned attack of hysterics.

She ran upstairs to the second floor, where her editorial office was located, grabbed a stamp-pad, and was prepared to rush off to Kitchener, catch the count, and take his fingerprints. It took a lot of persuading to calm her down, but she finally allowed herself to be comforted on Sheila's shoulder while I was left with the job of determining whether Count Trcka and Bignose were the same person.

I looked around for the telephone book but it was nowhere to be seen. Jirina noticed this over Sheila's shoulder and sobbed, "It's in the kitchen, but he gave me his number. It's in my purse over there, in my notebook."

The purse was lying on top of a pile of manuscripts beside a large ashtray that served as the final resting-place for a mountain of cigarette butts. Inside, I found a well-thumbed pocket diary, and under the letter T, the name and number. I dialled. No one answered. I let it ring for at least five minutes but there was no reply.

"What kind of hotel is this?" I exploded. "Twenty after eleven and there's no one there? Don't tell me they're sleeping in!"

"That number's not the main desk," said Jirina weakly. "That's his private number, to his apartment."

I stiffened. "Doesn't he live in the hotel?"

"He does, but he has a separate phone line to his private suite. So he said."

"Oh, shit," I said in a half-whisper. Who had my sister been talking to, then? Or could it have been that Trcka hadn't given her his private number?

10

Discoveries in Kitchener

It wasn't yet one o'clock when I walked into the Savoy. The trip cost me two speeding tickets but I was still driven by the sensation that some awful deadline was hanging over us. A minute later I was sitting at the hotel bar. This time the Czech monarch was absent, but Sheila had come along to make up for it. Partly to impress her, I spoke to the barman in a style I had absorbed from my reading of Chandler's *The Lady in the Lake*.

"I'll have two Scotch on the rocks and some information."

The bartender slowly put down a glass he was polishing and looked at me sharply. Perhaps he recognized me as that early drinker from two days earlier, because he glanced at his watch and, with an expressionless face, poured us two glasses of the house Scotch—the kind the government bottles—and then got ready to disappear.

"You've forgotten something," I said.

Very suspiciously, he slid a bowl of stale-looking almonds towards us.

"You can keep those," I said, beckoning him over with my finger.

Reluctantly, he leaned towards me across the bar. "I need some private information," I whispered confidentially. "If a young lady were to call your boss and your boss were in his apartment, could the call be transferred to him from the reception switchboard?"

The barman straightened up. I pulled three ten-dollar bills from my pocket and fanned them out on the bar. "This is for the whisky," I said, pointing to the first bill. "You can keep the change. This one is for your service, and the third is for any expenses you might incur."

He examined the bills thoughtfully. Then he picked them up and said, "Just a moment."

He disappeared. Sheila was staring past the bottles of vodka, Southern Comfort, Scotch, and rye at the portrait of Count Trcka.

"He can't be over fifty yet," Sheila said. "That nose might be the one we're after, but if Bignose looked thirty during the war he must be older than that. What's it been—thirty-two years?"

"Don't forget what Vogeltanz said," I reminded her. "People grow old fast in a war. Maybe the process gets reversed once the war's over. They relax, start living again, and begin to look younger."

"If it *is* him," said Sheila, "then he'd never be able to relax all that much."

That made sense, but I still pursued the point. "If it *is* him, he must have been a pretty tough customer."

"In that case he wouldn't have just *looked* thirty then."

Where age was concerned, Sheila simply had logic on her side. Feminine logic, perhaps.

A door behind the bar marked "Employees Only" opened, and the bartender came back, bringing with him a young man with light brown skin who was wearing a blue sports jacket with the word "Savoy" embroidered on the breast pocket.

"This is Jimmy, the receptionist," said the bartender laconically.

I repeated my question, and in a soft Caribbean accent Jimmy replied that calls through the central switchboard could not be transferred to Trcka's private apartment.

"What do you do when someone calls the hotel and wants to be put through to him?"

"We take a message."

"Isn't that a little inefficient?" asked Sheila. "And a pretty odd practice for a hotel with a live-in manager?"

The receptionist shrugged. "That's how the boss wants it. He doesn't want to be disturbed when he's not on the job. We're only allowed to call his apartment if there's some kind of emergency."

The young man's jacket was spotless and he was sporting a Duke Ellington moustache. I liked him. There was neither condescension nor hostility in his manner.

I thought for a moment. Calls could not be transferred to the count's suite from the central switchboard. A few weeks before her death, my sister had called the hotel at about midnight, when Trcka, in all probability, was deep in the privacy of his own apartment. So could she have been talking to Count Trcka at all? I turned to the receptionist. "Could I have a look at your records for the night of July 23, and for the fourth and fifth of August?"

"We can only give that kind of information out to the police, sir," said the young receptionist.

Sheila opened her purse and very deliberately took out her private investigator's licence. He looked at it skeptically, and then he studied Sheila even more skeptically. She blushed. She still didn't know how to deal with blatant sexism when it came from a member of an oppressed minority.

I placed another ten-dollar bill on top of the licence and the young man demonstrated nimbly enough that his race is in no way inferior to ours when it comes to responding to the charms of bribery. "Come to the reception desk, please," he said.

In a moment, an open ledger lay before us on the desk, while the receptionist discreetly turned his back and busied himself with something else. The hotel was thriving. It had forty rooms, and on the night of July 23, thirty-three of them had been occupied. On August 4, all of them had been full. There were several group bookings—one of them, I observed, was for the Friends of Genealogy from Lansing, Michigan—but when I eliminated those, the remaining list of guests was not uninteresting. Michael O'Donnell, Peggy O'Reilly, Thomas DeLuca, Patrick Solecki—a Slav?—William Barnett, Gustav Hall, Nikola Krsic—another Slavic name if ever there was one, but of course a woman and—Harrison Morrison....

Harrison Morrison?

My annoying friend from the Iroquois Racquet Club! My sister's long-distance admirer! In fact, his name appeared on the list twice: for July 23 and for the fourth of August.

Had I been wrong about his relationship with my sister? Yet the voice on the telephone had had an accent. But what if—

I pointed to the rhyming name with my finger and Sheila's eyes met mine.

As we were leaving the reception desk, Trcka strode into the hotel lobby. Sheila didn't notice him and I pretended not to. He was looking somewhat harried, and when he caught sight of me he seemed startled and turned abruptly into the restaurant. We left the hotel.

In the parking lot I told Sheila I was going to buy a paper and I walked back to the hotel, where an orange *Globe and Mail* box stood just outside the entrance. Through the glass doors I could see Trcka standing and talking to the receptionist about something. "Berating him" might be a better way of putting it, for even at that distance, I could see that it was an extremely emotional conversation.

"Neil, are you serious?" said Harrison Morrison.

He seemed genuinely shocked. He was dressed in one of those male bikinis and had been sitting in a deck chair a few yards from a huge private swimming pool cut into the side of a steep ravine. An inflatable mini-bar floated on the water and Harrison's plump wife was lying on it, absorbed in a crime novel. After checking to see that we hadn't disturbed his wife's concentration, Harrison invited us to come inside where it was cooler. He put on a beach robe, walked over to his domestic maxi-bar, and asked us what we'd like to drink. He looked worried.

Morrison's house—or, more precisely, his wife's house—overlooked the Don Valley, and a huge picture window in the living room afforded a panoramic view of the pool with his wife turning slowly on the plastic bar. Below her, in the distance, was the valley, its once-romantic river now hemmed in by a moving ribbon of traffic on the expressway. A police helicopter hung in the air like a huge dragonfly, suspended over a large bridge spanning the valley.

"You can't deny that you were her friend," said Sheila.

"Friend," said Harrison with bitterness in his voice, and looked cautiously out the window at his slowly revolving wife. "Why don't you say 'boyfriend', honey?" I was sure he'd used that last word just to make my detective girl angry. He succeeded.

"Well—were you her boyfriend?" she snapped.

"My relationship with Heather can hardly be expressed by that rather recent term. An old-fashioned word fits it much better: I was Heather's *admirer*." Harrison turned back to me. "You know perfectly well I never had anything going with your sister," he said, grinning ruefully. "It made me entirely unique among her male friends."

A wave of hatred for his cynicism poured over me. I looked around. There were some expensively upholstered leather chairs in an intimate grouping by the picture window. I walked over to them and Sheila followed me. I could hear Harrison's bare feet slapping excitedly on the parquet flooring behind us.

I stretched out in one of the chairs and took a drink of his whisky. He started to speak, but I cut him off. "That's exactly the point," I said.

This seemed to make him angry. "Listen, Neil, we've known each other for quite a while," he said evenly. "I'm not one to lose my head easily."

"Appearances can be deceiving. And besides, what you call your 'unique position' gives you a very solid motive."

He stood silently for a long time, looking out the window and sipping his drink. "I was fond of your sister, Neil," he said at last. "It hurt me more than anyone will ever know. I hid it by playing the cynic."

"Hurt you? That's another pretty solid motive, Harrison."

He gazed out the window at his wife floating on the blue water of the pool. "In books, maybe," he said. "The kind Megan devours with her whisky. Look, Neil, if it were in my nature, I'd have done it long ago, back when I was really hurting. But passion doesn't last for ever. When—when it happened—I no longer...I still had a soft spot for her, but...."

Outside, Harrison's wife had closed her novel and begun paddling the inflatable bar with her hands, aiming it at the ladder in the corner of the pool.

"What did you tell the police, Harrison?" I asked.

"Nothing."

"Bullshit!"

"They didn't even question me. She was the only one who knew about my old unrequited affection. And you." Harrison grinned. "And you only knew because I told you, remember?"

I remembered, all right. It was—how many?—three, four years ago? Harrison had confessed to me that he was hopelessly in love with Heather. At that time we were quite close. But when he failed to get anywhere with her he became a distant observer, a gossip-gatherer and a bore. Perhaps he was right. The police had no reason to suspect him, or even know about him.

By now his wife had reached the ladder. She peeled herself off the floating contraption with some difficulty, climbed heavily out of the pool, and plodded towards the house. She certainly did justice to the nourishing qualities of Limbo Springs Ale.

I couldn't shake off the unpleasant sensation that I was unjustly accusing Harrison. He looked at our glasses, noticed that Sheila's was empty like his own, reached for it. Sheila, still angry, was just about to refuse his services, but her addiction to the fiery water was stronger than her resentment. As Harrison was walking to the bar I looked at his muscular legs, broad shoulders, and rich blondish mane. He was a handsome man, and there was an odd dignity in him. If my sister wanted to know about life so badly, she could have done worse than to learn from him. Harrison was no intellectual, and he'd dropped out of university after three semesters, but he wasn't a cheat or a playboy or a frustrated sadist.

But I wondered: couldn't marriage to a beer heiress deepen a handsome young man's frustrations, despite the comfortable home in the best part of town, the swimming pool, the endless supply of Chivas Regal? Or did things like that happen only in detective novels?

Perhaps Sheila was reading my thoughts. Instead of thanking him for refreshing her drink she said icily, "Okay, granted you're not a very likely candidate. Still, have you got an alibi?"

He turned to face her and shook his head. "I don't suppose I have. I got back from Kitchener rather late that evening and Megan wasn't home yet. She was out somewhere—with the girls."

"There, you see?" she said. "You have a motive and you don't have an alibi. It may not be psychologically convincing, but it computes."

Harrison grimaced and turned back to me. "If it's logic you want, show me that list. I'm not the only one on it, am I?"

I hesitated, then handed it to him. "But you're the only one who knew my sister."

"Says who?"

I knew he was right; my assumption was groundless. Harrison studied the list we had compiled from the Savoy Hotel records. His wife came into the room, in her robe. Harrison quickly put the paper aside on the bar. "Like anything to drink, hun?"

"I'll mix my own," she replied, and walked over to the bottles, cutting Harrison off from the document.

"Well, what do you think of Wimbledon this year?" asked Harrison, rubbing his hands together rapidly. "I certainly didn't expect—"

"What's this list?" asked his wife idly.

Before Harrison could come up with an answer, I said, "One of those people may have killed my sister."

"Really?" she said and began to read the list aloud, for herself: "Michael O'Donnell...Peggy O'Reilly...."

"This is a man's murder, Mrs. Morrison," said Sheila. "You can skip Peggy O'Reilly and Nicole Krsic."

"Nicole Krsic?" interrupted Harrison.

Mrs. Morrison drank deeply from her glass of neat gin. Then she looked back at the list and added quickly, "But Harry, your name's here too!"

I looked rapidly at Harrison and saw that he was staring intently at his wife. He took the list from her.

"Neil's pulling your leg," he said. "This is just a list of people who were registered in the Savoy Hotel in Kitchener the day before his sister was killed. As you know, Megan, I go to Kitchener quite often to see Robinson, and I just happened to be there that day as well."

"What's being in Kitchener have to do with Neil's sister, for Christ's sake?" said Mrs. Morrison, taking another deep drink of undiluted gin before reaching for the tonic.

"Neil found out she made some phone calls to the hotel not long before she was killed."

"What does that prove?" she said. I could see she hadn't read all those detective novels for nothing.

"It's just another clue, hun," said Morrison.

"We haven't got a lot of leads," I said.

Harrison began reading the list out loud. He was as cool as a piece of ice now. "Michael O'Donnell, Peggy O'Reilly, Thomas DeLuca, Patrick Solecki, William Barnett, Gustav Hall, Nikola Krsic—*Nikola* Krsic...." He stopped. "Don't we know someone called Krsic, hun?"

The gin gurgled. "No. That is, I may. But only superficially. I think I met—someone like that—once, playing tennis at the McCormicks', it would have been—"

"Now I remember!" cried Harrison. "I was there with you— have you forgotten? But—isn't Nikola a *man*, hun?"

Mrs. Morrison made another gurgling sound.

"Yes, of course he is," continued Morrison with heavy irony. "He must have completely slipped your mind. Not Nicole, Nikola. Like Nikola Tesla, the famous inventor. Croatian or Albanian or whatever. A dark-skinned, black-eyed hunk of a macho."

Megan again resorted to her gin. It was obvious that the beer magnate's daughter would have loved to change the subject.

"Or are his eyes blue?" said Harrison. "I don't remember him that well either. Anyway—what about this year's Wimbledon?"

We talked about Wimbledon.

When we left, Harrison walked us out to the car and his wife went back to cool herself off, both internally and externally, at her floating bar. Sheila got in the car and Harrison put his hand on my shoulder.

"Do you remember the day they told you the news? At the Racquet Club?"

I looked at him questioningly. He was being serious. "I talked like a jerk, forgive me, but what I said was true. I saw your sister in the Four Seasons with a black-haired chap with dark eyes and a mangled nose."

I nodded, waiting.

"What I didn't tell you was that I knew who he was. It seemed better—at that point—to make it sound a little mysterious. But I know him. And I saw him again recently, in the lobby of the Savoy Hotel—that day—when I was settling my bill. He certainly isn't your average WASP. From the Balkans, I'd say. Think of the names on that list."

It wasn't difficult to recall: the same name that had caused Mrs. Morrison some embarrassment. Harrison was clearly taking an interest in this Mr. Krsic as well, I thought. I had an idea.

"How would you like to come along with us, Harrison?"

He hesitated. "Why?" he said suspiciously.

"Krsic may try to deny that he ever knew my sister, and you actually saw them together."

"Is that all?"

"What other reason could there possibly be?" I asked.

11

The Wife

The address wasn't hard to trace. After all, how many Krsics are there in the phone book? It was a place in Thornhill, so we drove across the Bloor viaduct and down the ramp onto the Don Valley Parkway to join the thickening late-afternoon traffic. There was a thin, barely visible haze above the valley, and the air was foul and sticky.

Mrs. Krsic was at home alone. She had raven-black hair and jet-black eyebrows that met over the bridge of a magnificent aquiline nose. But this took nothing away from her beauty. Her skin was even darker than the receptionist's at the Savoy, and she was draped in a pink robe under which I assumed she was wearing a bathing suit, for she came to the door in her bare feet. She looked as though she'd spent the afternoon by the pool.

I'll say this much for her: she did have a sense of humour. As soon as we asked about her husband she said, "Well, well, all male enquiries today." She looked at me and then, with much more interest, at Harrison. "What in the world has Nikola been up to? Or are you asking on behalf of your wife?" And she turned her black eyes towards Sheila.

"I'm not his wife," said Sheila testily.

"That happens too. So—is it *your* better half, handsome?" She turned to Harrison.

He darkened.

"Certainly not!"

"I wouldn't be so certain," said Mrs. Krsic, "if I were you. Nikola's a very accomplished serpent." She looked back at me. "Well, who is the little goose?"

That took my breath away.

"Come on, there's nothing to be afraid of. Nothing will happen to *her*. I always settle my accounts with Nikola alone. The poor little girls can't help it. Look at me. I couldn't help it either."

The figure beneath the bathrobe appeared to be statuesque. Nikola probably paid dearly for each of his little adventures. I should have checked first to see if Krsic was married, but so far none of the suspects had been. I explained to Mrs. Krsic that we had reason to believe her husband knew my sister.

"Is she knocked up?" she asked matter-of-factly. "If she is she's out of luck, because Nikola can't afford any more support payments. And my poor late father was smarter than I was—the house and all our paper assets are in my name. According to my father's will, I can't turn any of it over to Nikola, and I can tell you that after ten years of happily married life I'm grateful for my father's wisdom."

"Neil's sister is dead, Mrs. Krsic," said Sheila coldly. "She was murdered."

"Is that so?" said the suntanned woman calmly. "I'm relieved to hear it."

We were speechless. The woman's next remark was even more astonishing. "In that case, Nikola has nothing to worry about."

"Just the opposite, wouldn't you say?" retorted Harrison.

She shook her head. "He's even more afraid of God than he is of me. He's a true Croatian, a pillar of the faith. He believes literally in that story about the rib in the Garden of Eden. And

Nikola has more experience with what the Lord made of it than Casanova himself."

"Then isn't he afraid God will punish him for his philandering?" said Sheila.

"You see, dear," said the lady patiently, "Nikola's God is a very human God. Minor sins like fornication are easily washed away in confession. But murder? That's another story. Look, I know Nikola. You're wasting your time. I'm sorry about your sister, but I wouldn't be surprised if she had some other men in her life too. Now if you'll excuse me," and she began to close the door.

Quickly I asked, "All the same, couldn't we talk to your husband? Perhaps he knows someone who knew her."

"Not today," said the dynamic lady. "He was at his office earlier, but he said he was going out of town on business this afternoon." She winked. "On business."

And she closed the door in my face.

We went back to the car. Suddenly I remembered something. How had she put it? I told Sheila and Harrison to wait and went back to the front door and rang the bell a second time. Deep inside the house a set of chimes tinkled a dinky little melody. A fountain was splashing in the garden, and beyond it I could see the cobalt-blue waters of a swimming pool.

The door opened and the lady appeared again. This time she was wearing a dazzling gold two-piece bathing suit. She was a little too olympian for my taste, but she definitely wasn't someone you could ignore.

"That didn't take long," she said. "Come on in. If you want a bathing suit, Nikola's is hanging in the bathroom."

"I'm sorry, I can't come in," I said, somewhat flustered. "I only wanted to ask you—"

The brown face registered mild disappointment. "You could put her in touch with Nikola. She's quite pretty."

99

I ignored her crack, which for all I know she may have meant seriously, and continued, "I only wanted to know if anyone else besides me has been asking about your husband today."

"Hmm," she said. "So today is out, is it?"

"Today is out," I replied firmly.

"Well, you know where to find me. Yes, as a matter of fact someone did ask, a Mr. Chumac. He called about two, wanted to talk to Nikola, so I gave him his office number. It's just possible he may have caught up with him before he left. Was that really all you wanted?"

"Yes, that's all, thanks," I replied. "Have a good day."

"You're not helping," she said, and for the second time closed the door in my face.

We drove off in silence through the gently rolling countryside north of Toronto, gradually descending to the lake. The sun dropping towards the west cast long shadows across the land. The golden air, heavy with nostalgia, bathed the August-green fields surrounded by wire fences bearing No Trespassing signs. Silver silos stood erect on scattered farms like monuments to a vanishing age, linking heaven to earth. Some of the farms had already been abandoned to developers, who had left the barns to collapse in heaps of silvery lumber.

I began to think about my kid sister again, but Sheila was droning on about Croatian nationalists and how they had all been dirty little Fascists ever since the war. Gradually Sheila's lesson in history intruded on my memories of Heather, conjuring up a vision of that scene on the steppes of the Ukraine. A man whose chief distinguishing feature was a huge nose. A man who after the war, in the interests of his own survival, had to blend into the anonymous masses of people fleeing the powers of the East, escaping to lands just purged of a similar power in the West. A handful among those hundreds of thousands of refugees had been agents of that defeated power, and they knew that the victor in the East would show them no mercy.

But what about those agents who stayed behind? Hadn't I heard somewhere that a number of ex-Nazis were now living snugly in Eastern Europe, not as prisoners but as reliable servants of the new regime? Could they have been anything else, with the threat of a deadly blackmail? "Your past is safe with us, Comrade, as long as you do what we say." Would any government extend that privilege to Gestapo murderers? Could any regime be that cynical?

I turned on the radio to catch the seven o'clock news. There was no mention of Heather—she was already gone and forgotten, supplanted by headlines of an impending transit strike, and the escape of a pack of baboons from the zoo.

The sun touched the horizon and a long shadow spread across the landscape, while the towers of downtown Toronto shimmered in the last golden rays. Summer was squandering its final beauties upon us. Why, in the midst of this serenity, was I haunted by the feeling that we were working against an unknown deadline?

12

Late at Night

We found the editor of *Toronto Lady* proof-reading the next issue of her magazine over a half-empty bottle of Liebfraumilch. Two more bottles stood on the floor in the shadow of her writing table. One of them was uncorked and looked empty; no doubt this issue would be bristling with typographical errors. She took the half-empty bottle and the four of us went into the living room, where we were joined by the cat, who obviously loved company. Once again, he very cleverly positioned himself in the stream of cool air flowing from the air conditioner.

"Jirina," I said when she had poured us drinks, "I'm still not clear on what happened to those fingerprints after the war. And to Bignose, for that matter. What did the Czechs actually do with their collaborators?"

Jirina looked at me inquisitively. "I was only a baby then," she said, "but yes, let me try to piece it together for you."

And she told us the story of her obsession. It seems that neither her courageous mother nor old Inspector Vodicka, to whom she had entrusted the fingerprints, survived the war. Fortunately, however, Vodicka was wise in the ways of the world. He sealed the prints in an envelope and gave them to a lawyer, instructing him to try, with the utmost discretion, to discover whether any Czechs or Germans accused of collaboration after the war could be identified as Bignose. Failing that, the envelope was to be turned over to Jirina when she was eighteen.

The lawyer failed to carry out the first part of his commission because, as the old police inspector had foreseen, the Ministry of the Interior, and hence the police, came under Communist control right after the war, and in a number of the collaboration trials the Party was able to manipulate evidence to ensure that its enemies were eliminated and its potential new allies protected. Even with friends in the judiciary, the lawyer, who was a social democrat, was unable to discover whether anyone resembling Bignose had been brought to trial.

The lawyer's discretion was well enough developed to help him survive the Communist purges after 1948, though not as a lawyer. He ended his days as a stoker in the boiler room of a large hotel in downtown Prague. In 1959 he carried out the second half of his commission, as instructed. And so Jirina, who could remember neither of her parents, learned for the first time what her mother had done seventeen years before. This was the first time the fingerprints had seen the light of day.

If the old inspector had been distrustful of the new police force, Jirina had come to hate them; a boyfriend of hers had died in a uranium mine under police jurisdiction. So she could not bring herself to turn the evidence over to them or to go to them for help. In any case, interest in war crimes had suddenly died the day the Party assumed absolute power and crimes against the state became all the rage. So Jirina kept the fingerprints and harboured the romantic notion of singlehandedly tracking down the monster with the huge nose. There had even been a time, she said, when she imagined herself an agent of divine justice, and she had been quite prepared, then, to kill in order to avenge her father.

The problem was that she had no idea how to conduct a search on her own. There were of course no private investigation agencies left in Czechoslovakia (here Jirina looked significantly at Sheila), and asking too many questions would have brought more suspicion down on her than on the object of her search. So her chances of finding Bignose dwindled to nothing, and gradually her rage subsided and her secret became just another Czech yarn.

"How many people know this story, Jirina?" I asked when she had finished. "Did you ever tell Herman about it?"

"I haven't mentioned it to him for at least ten years, if not more," said Jirina, "and that was back in Prague. By the time I left for Montreal, we had already—"

She stopped. That annoying habit of hers again.

"Were you and Herman close friends before you came to Canada?" Sheila asked.

Was it the light, or was the usually brash editor of *Toronto Lady* actually blushing?

"Well, as a matter of fact we were," she said. "But before I left for Expo '67, we had more or less split up."

"When did he come to Canada, then?"

Jirina told us how, about a year after Expo, Herman had washed ashore in Canada on the shock waves set in motion by the Soviet tanks that occupied Prague that summer. But was the invasion the only reason? Hadn't he merely taken advantage of that unexpected opportunity to get out of the country and follow his beloved?

"People come here for all sorts of reasons," said Jirina. She got up rather unsteadily and left the room. The cat got to its feet on the television set, stretched itself into an inverted "U", jumped down onto the carpet, and padded silently after its mistress. Sheila looked at me. Harrison was busy examining the spines of the books in Jirina's extensive library. Half of them were incomprehensible.

"Jirina," I said when she had come back and the cat had jumped into her lap, "did you take up with McCavish before you'd really broken up with Herman?"

The owner of *Toronto Lady* took a deep drink of her wine. "All right, yes, I did," she said. "And Herman made a scene when he showed up in Canada, and who can blame him? We were more or less engaged before I left Czechoslovakia. It wasn't official or anything, but I'd divorced my former husband because of him and he had a right to believe I was serious. But how was I to know I'd meet McCavish in Montreal? Anyway, Herman moved out west and we lost touch. Then he came back to Toronto a couple of years ago. By that time his ardour had cooled and we were just friends." She took another drink. "But I'll tell you something frankly. If I'd known Heather intended to spend the night with Herman, I don't think I'd have let her stay here." She spoke evenly, with unexpected intensity.

I shook my head while the implications crowded in on me. If she had refused, they would probably have gone to a hotel or to Herman's place. Would the murderer—if he was looking for Heather—have found her there?

Herman had been looking for Krsic earlier today, and Krsic was in all probability the man Heather had talked to, more than once, at the Savoy Hotel. Herman also knew in detail the story of Jirina's search for revenge. Who had mistaken whom?

It was another hot night and the semi-liquid air poured in the window of the BMW like hot syrup. I closed the windows and turned on the air conditioner. When we reached the Old English Pub it was just a few minutes shy of ten forty-five.

Herman wasn't there. The head waiter told us that at about seven that evening he had left for Kitchener. I rushed to the telephone and dialled long distance on my Bell card. The phone rang a few times, and then the very proper voice of the young West Indian receptionist said, "Savoy Hotel."

"This is Neil Donby here. You may recall—"

"Yes, Mr. Donby."

"Do you happen to know the manager of the Old English Pub in Toronto?"

"I do, sir."

Strange. The receptionist did, the boss didn't.

"Have you seen him today?"

"Yes, he passed through the lobby. I haven't seen him since. Oh, and by the way, Mr. Donby," and the voice, though polite, held a perceptible reproach, "I had a very unpleasant incident with the boss over that little favour I did for you this morning. He threatened to fire me."

"I'll straighten it out with him," I said reassuringly. "Is your boss there now?"

"He's gone to bed already and doesn't want to be disturbed."

"Then I'll explain it to him later. And I'll make all this worth your while, I promise you."

There was a moment of silence, then he said without the slightest trace of sarcasm, "I'm at your service, as usual."

"There is something else, Jimmy. Do you remember a man called Nikola Krsic? He usually stays at the Savoy when he's in Kitchener."

"Yes, as a matter of fact he's registered with us today. Room 305."

I took a deep breath. "Is he in his room now? Or has he gone out?"

"His key isn't here. But guests sometimes keep their keys when they go out. Shall I try to ring through to him for you?"

"No, Jimmy. I want to confront—to see him in person. I'm driving out there right now. If he goes out, could you try to find where he's off too? Without mentioning me, of course."

The receptionist agreed. I hung up and turned to Sheila and Harrison. Harrison had come with us this far out of curiosity, and now he was anxious to get home. When I told him what I'd learned, he changed his mind. He tied up the phone for the next ten minutes, while we watched him from the car. He appeared to be having a heated debate with someone. It wasn't hard to guess with whom.

The night refused to cool off. As we sped along the 401, I turned the air conditioner up full. We were all absorbed in trying to find answers to a growing number of questions and we didn't realize how chilly we'd become. When we arrived at the Savoy and got out of the car, the wave of heat nearly knocked us out. It was an hour past midnight and a sense of imminent disaster hung in the thick air—or perhaps it was just an impending storm.

The lobby was deserted except for the receptionist, who was standing behind the counter going over the day's receipts. He seemed just as rested as he had that afternoon, though they were obviously working him overtime. He looked, if anything, more dignified than usual in his spotless blue sports coat.

With graceful ease he picked up the twenty-dollar bill I offered him and said, "Either Mr. Krsic hasn't come back yet or he's in his room. I didn't want to call him, especially at this time of night. But you're welcome to try."

"Where's the house telephone?" I asked.

He pointed around the corner. The telephone was blood-red. I dialled the room number, let it ring a few times, and just when I was about to hang up a voice full of sleepy irritation answered, "What's going on?"

"Mr. Krsic?" Was it the same voice that had talked to my sister? I couldn't be sure.

"Who's this?"

"Neil Donby. I have to talk with you right away, about something urgent."

"Never heard of you," said the voice gruffly. Then he invited me to go to hell.

"After what you did to my sister, you may well be going there yourself," I retorted. I was surprised at my own directness. In the last few days—perhaps influenced by the same literary sources that had put that bottle in Sheila's desk—I had become more professional.

For a long time Krsic said nothing. His brain was battling, either with sleep or with something worse.

"I don't know what you're talking about," he said finally.

Silence again. He was probably trying to figure out how much I already knew. "I don't have a clue who your sister is or what you think I've done."

"Look," I said firmly, "I have witnesses who saw you with my sister. If you won't see me now, I'm calling the police."

After another pause he said, "I still don't know what you're talking about, but I suppose you'd better come up."

So we did. I asked Harrison to remain out of sight in the hall.

"Why? I'd like to see the bastard," he growled, with deep and genuine feeling. I wondered whether the source of it was Heather or Megan, and suddenly the whole thing struck me as rather theatrical. But I dismissed that impression.

"You're the only one who saw them together," I said. "He'll probably start by denying that he knew Heather. So I want to have a surprise in store for him."

Harrison accepted that, though without much enthusiasm. Sheila and I went to the door and I knocked.

Krsic opened the door. He was wearing a pair of silk pyjamas with short trousers and a maple-leaf pattern on them, and he had a Florida tan. He was certainly fifty, probably more. But the stout legs emerging from his pyjama trousers were free of varicose veins and he had the biceps of a boxer. A tattoo that looked like an eagle adorned his right wrist. It was holding something in its talons. And on his head he was wearing an item of gentleman's apparel I'd only seen in those old comedies of the thirties: a hairnet.

But the most outstanding thing about him was his nose. It may not have been aquiline, but it was certainly large. It had a wide bridge, then it dipped unnaturally like a saddle and finished in a sharp point that seemed to belong to another nose altogether.

Krsic gestured impatiently towards two armchairs and sat down on the edge of the bed. The silk trousers revealed the outline of a sexual organ of astonishing dimensions. "What did you say your name was?" he asked. "And who's this dame?" He nodded towards Sheila.

"My name is Donby," I said. "This lady is Sheila Sullivan—she's a private detective. And my sister's name was Heather."

He rubbed his eyes with the finger and thumb of one hand and said nothing. Was he waking up or trying to refresh his memory? According to what his wife had said, Heather would have been just one of many casual affairs.

"You've come to the wrong place," he said finally, "you and your private dick. I don't know your sister."

It sounded insolent, but not convincing.

"Were you in this hotel the night of the fourth or fifth of August?" asked Sheila sharply.

"Quite possibly. I often stay here."

"And on the night of the twenty-third of July?"

"Maybe. I don't keep a diary."

"On both those nights my sister talked on the phone to someone in this hotel," I said. "Whoever it was had a Slavic accent, like yours."

He stared at me intently with his crow-black eyes. "I'm not the only one in Canada with a Slavic accent," he said drily.

"No one's saying you are," I replied, and paused. "But there can't be many noses like yours running around the country."

Once again he scrutinized me carefully. "Look, let me give you some advice. Get the hell out of here, you and your—whatever she is. It's late and I have to get some sleep. I don't know who put all these crazy ideas in your head, but it has definitely not been

110

my pleasure to meet you." He stood up and motioned towards the door with a muscular arm.

I nodded to Sheila and she went to the door and opened it. Harrison was standing on the threshold and without waiting to be asked, he walked into the room.

Krsic glared at him and said, "Look here, I've had enough of this bloody melodrama. If you don't clear out right now, I'm throwing you out."

"If you'll just be patient for a moment," I said, "this is Mr. Harrison Morrison. Even if you can't remember my sister, perhaps you can recall a name like that."

It was a shot in the dark, my only basis for it being the strange turn of conversation between the Limbo Springs heiress and Harrison earlier in the afternoon, concerning the person who was not Nicole but Nikola.

Nikola Krsic stiffened, but Harrison rose to the occasion. "Well, so this is Mr. Krsic."

Krsic crossed his arms across his huge, gorilla-like chest and set his feet a little farther apart. He was probably thinking, correctly, that this time denial would be more difficult. Harrison, unlike me, gave the impression that he was on solid ground.

Also, murder wasn't the issue here. Krsic employed the old trick of confessing to stealing a penny to hide the theft of a dollar.

Harrison was at least a head taller than Krsic. He took up a similar stance and said, "All right, let's hear it."

"There's nothing to say," said Krsic, who was beginning to look somewhat chastened. "Not much, anyway. I—"

"Where did you meet her?"

"Look, Mr. Morrison, I can't help it if—"

"I said where did you pick her up?"

"In the lounge of the Four Seasons," said Krsic somewhat guiltily. "I don't know what—"

"There, you see?" Harrison turned to me. "What did I tell you?"

"I do see," I said. "Mr. Krsic obviously has a regular hunting ground. Heather didn't go there very often, and when she did she had to run into a creep like this." I was being insanely cocky, but Harrison's presence was reassuring.

"Heather?" said Krsic uncertainly. His dark eyes jumped from Harrison to me and back again. He was trying to decide which tack would be safer. The fact that he chose to deal with me didn't bode well for our hypothesis.

"Yes, Heather," I said. "My sister. My dead sister."

He looked me in the eyes, then turned away.

"She didn't die a natural death," said Sheila.

He squinted towards the night table, where a pocket flask stood. He was clearly struggling with himself and the struggle must have been a powerful one. Chandler was right: whenever a man fights the bottle, the bottle always wins. And it did now.

"She called you from Mrs. McCavish's house," I said, "and asked you to come and be with her. She told you she'd be there alone. And that night she was murdered."

He put the bottle back on the table and looked at me, this time straight into my eyes. They were as black as Lethe.

"I didn't kill your sister, Mr. Donby," he said intensely. "I swear to God, I didn't kill her."

Once again he looked at the night table. Beside the pocket flask lay a hotel Bible. Would he pick it up? He didn't.

"You're right, she did ask me to come. I refused. She—she got very upset and hysterical. I'd been trying to break it off with her. But I couldn't kill anyone, Mr. Donby. I'd rather face up to the consequences, do you understand what I mean?" Then he added in tragic tones, "Man is a vessel of weakness, Mr. Donby. If you want, you can hit me. I deserve it. But I did not kill Heather."

The next thing I knew, he was offering me his cheek in a biblical gesture that afforded me an excellent view of his strange nose. For a moment I struggled with a strong temptation to comply, but I restrained myself.

Harrison, however, did not.

His blow spun Krsic around a hundred and eighty degrees and the big man fell forward on the bed. I expected to see him leap back into action like an affronted cowboy in an American Western. Harrison couldn't be the first modern husband to react to a cuckolding in the old-fashioned manner, and I assumed that Krsic was experienced in fighting such duels.

Oddly enough, however, as soon as he had recovered from the blow, he stood up and offered Harrison, who was standing at the ready with his fists up like a boxer, his other cheek. His wife hadn't been exaggerating.

"Hit me!" he said melodramatically. "I deserve it and I apologize to you."

Harrison has never fought with anyone who wouldn't fight back. He let his hands drop to his sides, spat symbolically, and took a less dramatic way out. "Go to hell, Krsic," he said, and swigged an uninvited drink from the bedside flask.

Then we gave the humbled Casanova a grilling.

"Do you know Herman Chumac?"

"Yes. He was here this evening. He wanted to know—the same as you, basically."

"Did you know about Herman and my sister?"

"No."

"I don't believe you."

Krsic reached for the Bible this time. "Forget it," said Harrison. "It's a Protestant Bible and God, as you know, is Catholic."

Krsic pulled his hand back gingerly. His nose caught my eye again.

"What happened to that?" I said, pointing to the unnatural protuberance.

"I was in the war. The resistance. This," he said, pointing to his nose, "is a souvenir of a rifle-butt."

"A German rifle?" asked Sheila.

He didn't answer. Sheila moved to the offensive. "Why did you leave Yugoslavia after the war? The partisans won, didn't they?"

His dark eyes almost stabbed my girl. "I was in the other resistance. And anyway," and he turned back to me, "it has nothing to do with your sister's death."

At that moment, I wasn't so sure any more.

We walked along the corridor to the elevator. The doors in the dimly lit passage had gold numbers on them, and thin panes of imitation Tiffany glass over the door frames.

"A Fascist," whispered Sheila. "In Yugoslavia there were units that basically collaborated with the Nazis." She looked at me. "With the Gestapo...."

"But Bignose was a Czech," whispered Harrison. "And anyway, that doesn't mean that everyone—"

"Are we really sure he's Croatian?" Sheila interrupted. "Can you tell by his accent? Or his looks?"

"It's what his wife said."

"But she met him years after the war. She said she'd only known him for ten years."

The need to vanish into the anonymity of the masses. Which is easier, changing one's nationality or changing one's distinguishing features? And supposing one were to do both? Is there such a difference between Czechs and Croatians that—?

And what did any of this have to do with Heather?

Was it, as Mr. Boruvka had suggested all along, a genuine mistake?

I was overcome by the feeling that we had set out on a stormy sea without knowing how to sail. We reached the end of the corridor and discovered that the elevators were at the opposite end. We walked back. Over the last door a weak wash of coloured light flowed into the hall through the Tiffany glass. Where the room number should have been there was a shiny plaque that said:

MANAGER'S APARTMENT
PRIVATE

Trcka! Why were his lights on so late at night? Was he still up? Or had he fallen asleep and forgotten to turn them off?

Sheila and Harrison looked at the plaque. I knocked.

Nothing. Only silence.

I knocked again.

Then I pounded.

Finally, I kicked at the door.

But no sound came from the room. There was only that light from above, shining weakly through the Tiffany glass, casting a wide band of colour on the ceiling.

I looked at Sheila and Sheila looked at me. We both looked at Harrison.

"Lift me up," whispered Sheila.

Harrison and I took her by the arms and slowly lifted her until she could peer through the multi-coloured pane of glass. Her face turned blue, with a slash of red across her neck. We could feel her shudder.

"You can let me down now," she said.

We set her down lightly on the carpet. She looked pale in the gloom of the hallway.

"He's in there," she said. "I think he's had it."

He had. He was slumped in a chair by a glass coffee table with a bottle of Remy Martin standing by it. His eyes were open, staring into the distance. His mouth was twisted in an ugly grimace. His prominent nose was pointed towards the ceiling. On its side, next to the chair, lay an empty glass.

The receptionist, who had let us in, felt for his pulse but immediately drew back. I took Trcka's wrist in my hand. It was cool with the chill of death. The room was cold. The air conditioner was turned on full.

The deadline was past.

13

Robbery

Until the next morning, my experience with the police—except for speeding tickets, which I always deserved—had been positive. For that matter, the grilling I got now was deserved as well. I shouldn't have hired Sheila and her watchful sisters in the first place. Even without a murder case, the business would have prospered—and then died a natural death when its owner lost interest in detection. Eventually she would have developed a passion for native art and opened a gallery on Queen Street. Or she might suddenly have found the idea of matriarchy attractive and decided, against all odds, for marriage, perhaps with me. No, I should have stuck to my guns—that is, to my office, my cars, my squash, and my cigars—and let the police handle the whole affair by themselves.

The interrogation in Kitchener was an ordeal, and Sheila got the worst of it. The officer from the Homicide Squad behaved impeccably, having obviously been trained in the British tradition rather than in the American school of TV cop-show tactics, but his sophisticated irony hurt her more than churlish ridicule would have. He was a male chauvinist of the most reactionary, which is to say the most intelligent, variety. We had to tell him the embarrassing truth: that in the course of our investigation we had come upon several circumstances that Sheila was bound, by the conditions laid down in her private investigator's licence, to report to the police immediately. Instead, she had only reported the final event—the death of Dusan Trcka—because it was hardly possible to keep that a secret.

One thing we did manage to keep secret, though—the business of Nikola. We both stuck to our story, which after all was not untrue, that we had come to Kitchener to have a word with Trcka. I told the police we'd been investigating a hunch that my sister's murder was a mistake. The inspector listened impassively while I told him Jirina's yarn about her father's murderer, the fingerprints, and her own private quest for revenge. Then I told him about the poor old boy who thougnt he was the King of Bohemia, and suggested that they might look in Trcka's background for evidence of fraud. This seemed to interest him more. I could see he didn't place much stock in my vague hypothesis about Jirina being the real target—tales of Balkan spies and smuggled scandal were a little out of his line—but fraud was something he could understand because it was a product of ordinary human greed.

The police weren't through with us until breakfast. They took their time, especially with Harrison. He tried to explain his presence by describing himself as a gentleman adventurer who, besides having been a friend of all the participants in the case for many years, was particularly attracted by the Balkan aspect of it. He was, he asserted, an incurable addict of spy fiction. That was true of his wife but not of him, and it brought heavy suspicion down on his head. It appeared that one of the squad was an addict, and from time to time the interrogation changed into something like an oral exam of a pathetically under-prepared freshman.

They let us go just before breakfast, and told us in confidence that Trcka had died of cyanide poisoning—a decidedly aristocratic way to go, I thought—and that they were inclined to treat it as suicide. They wouldn't know for sure until the banks opened, they said, but from personal papers left in his apartment, he appeared to have been rather heavily in debt. To whom, they could not (or would not) say.

They also told us that they were going to review Sheila's private investigator's licence and that we shouldn't be surprised if it was revoked.

On the drive back to Toronto, I suddenly realized I'd forgotten to mention that Herman, their prime suspect in my sister's murder, had spent the night in the Savoy Hotel. In a way I was glad I'd forgotten. Things were complicated enough as it was. If Herman had anything at all to do with this fiasco, he'd be more use to us at liberty than behind bars.

I turned what I knew over in my mind. I was dying to think out loud, and to get Sheila's reactions, but she was sound asleep in the back seat. I went over everything we knew by myself, trying to fit this motley assembly of characters and events into some kind of pattern. It was no use. Either my logic was faulty, or there was something we needed to know before we could make sense of all the rest. I concluded that it was time to check out some fingerprints. Perhaps Sue's father could help. He at least should know something about the workings of the Central European criminal mind, if that was in fact what we were dealing with.

The rest of the way back, I thought of Sue McLaughlin.

It was after lunch. The broadloom in Sheila's office felt like muskeg under foot and outside the wide window downtown Toronto was perspiring so profusely that the lower half of the CN Tower was veiled in haze.

Harrison had gone home, probably to get some sleep and have words with the heiress of Limbo Springs.

Sheila's air conditioner had given out, overburdened by the heat and the non-stop service, and the air in her office was like a Chinese laundry.

"I'm at my wits' end," said Sheila with unaccustomed frankness. "I haven't a clue what to do now."

"Do you suppose Mr. Boruvka knows anything about fingerprinting?" I wondered.

Sheila looked at me. "Let's give him a call," she said. "I think it's time for a conference."

It was a significant moment. Here was an emissary of feminine superiority turning for help to a man she quite justifiably suspected of being a reactionary. I looked out the window at the CN Tower poking through the steaming miasma that enveloped the lower city. It occurred to me that the parking-lot attendant had probably never been outside Toronto, except for that obligatory trip to Niagara Falls, so I called the CN Tower, managed (to my surprise) to reserve a window table for supper, then called Jirina and Mr. Boruvka.

He had just come off his shift. I warned him that he had to wear a tie and leave his jeans at home if he wanted to dine at the top of Toronto, but after I hung up I realized that I'd never seen him in anything but a suit and tie.

The waterfront fell away from under us with a sickening tilt as the glass box shot up the outside of the tower. Above the mist and to the east across Lake Ontario, an enormous thundercloud was rolling towards us. Jirina clung to the wall behind the elevator operator, but Mr. Boruvka and his daughter stood right by the glass door, looking down and talking in that mysterious, melodic tongue that sounds like a pleasant but incomprehensible waterfall.

Sheila leaned into my shoulder. She was exhausted. I wasn't feeling too perky myself, and I almost regretted arranging this dinner party before we'd had a chance to recover from the previous day's escapades. My ears popped and cleared and I was just beginning to admire the view and forget my own weariness when the conveyance whooshed to a stop, forcing my stomach into my rib-cage.

This was the first time I'd managed to be seated at a window table. The few times I'd been there before, I'd always been stashed away at one of the tables at the back, away from the touristy sight of my native city. But now we were watching Toronto revolve slowly beneath us. The city was blanketed with low cloud, and the sensation was something like hanging aloft in a balloon. Here and there the office towers poked through the cotton batten below us, and in the distance we could see tall apartments belonging to Cadillac Fairview. Or maybe to oil barons with villas on the Gulf of Aqaba. As the wind rose, patches of residential neighbourhoods became visible, set off by deep green gashes of ravine—as though the primordial Ontario forest, with its raccoons and skunks and foxes—and now, perhaps, baboons—were bursting through the concrete shell of the city.

When I'm with visitors from out of town, I have a tendency to belittle Toronto by saying it's just a big village. This is especially true when I have visitors from Europe, who are used to grander and more ancient cities. So today I tried to provoke our rather anxious group into conversation by claiming that the view from the CN Tower was uninteresting. Our cathedrals no longer dominate the landscape, I said, and the only castle in view— Casa Loma, the mad dream of a demented millionaire—is really a glorified gym, home to fund-raising parties and senior proms.

But Mr. Boruvka gazed in awe at the city slowly rotating beneath him, and declared that it was beautiful. Sue said, somewhat mysteriously, that in any case baroque architecture was beautiful only to the eye. I couldn't understand what she meant—perhaps that inside those beautiful ancient buildings the facilities were woefully inadequate.

As the detective and his daughter gazed out over the city, the grim weather front, with looming black thunderheads as outriders, seemed to be rolling in. Perhaps the weather was going to break at last. I realized with annoyance that I'd left my umbrella at home.

Sheila was anxious to get down to business. As soon as we'd ordered, she told the others what had happened the night before, in Kitchener, and explained the conclusions she had come to. Trcka, she reasoned, had murdered my sister, probably out of jealousy, but he wasn't a hardened killer so he'd suffered a breakdown and, in a fit of remorse, had taken his own life. As she always did when making deductions, Sheila ignored what didn't suit her hypothesis. Mr. Boruvka listened to her politely and nodded respectfully as she made her points. If he had any objections, he didn't raise them.

Until it came to the cyanide. Many before Trcka had chosen to end their own lives that way, and yet—

"A poison like cyanide," said the former police lieutenant, "is not normally very available. I don't know how it is in Canada, but I don't believe it can be very different here than in—"

"It's not impossible to come by," I said, because Sheila didn't reply. "But it's true that cyanide's not like marijuana."

"Besides that, if you will permit me another question," he continued, "did the policemen find the ampoule? Cyanide is usually in sealed glass ampoules, because it is a very volatile and quick poison. If Mr. Trcka put cyanide in his cognac, he would have to break the end off the ampoule and leave it somewhere. Of course, maybe he used a plastic ampoule and swallowed it. Or maybe he threw the ampoule out of the window or put it down the toilet before he drank the cognac. But why would he do that if he was committing suicide?"

"I'll ask Bill Kendrick if they found anything," Sheila said a little grudgingly. "The officer who interrogated us didn't mention an ampoule, but he was under no obligation to tell us anything."

"It might also be good," the detective continued, "to show a photograph of Mr. Trcka to Mr. von Vogeltanz. You said you wanted to bring them together. Now it is impossible, of course, but a good photograph—"

I reached into my pocket. The brochure from the Savoy Hotel was still there, and I smoothed it out on the table in front of Mr. Boruvka. He studied the likeness carefully for some time.

God knows what Mr. Boruvka was trying to divine from Trcka's supernaturally sparkling dentures, or from that silvered moustache and those flawless features whose wrinkles had been so carefully airbrushed. Or was he trying to penetrate his secrets by communing with that prominent nose? Whatever it was, he took his time about it. Sue studied the count's face over her father's shoulder. Somewhere in the distance, thunder rumbled faintly. I felt a sense of imminent relief. The storm would come after all.

The detective looked up at Sheila. "I think Mr. von Vogeltanz should see this. And if you'll permit, there's no time to waste." Something in his voice chilled me. Was another deadline hanging over us?

"I'll call him," said Sue. "He may be at home, on a Sunday. Should I ask him to come here?"

"If that is possible."

The detective's daughter stood up and walked towards the washrooms, where there were several public telephones. Mr. Boruvka turned to Jirina. "Also, if you'd be so kind, might I see the fingerprints?"

"Certainly." The editor reached for her purse, felt around next to her chair for a moment, and then looked under it. "Oh my God!" she exclaimed. "I put my handbag down here beside me. And now I can't find it!"

We looked all around, with no luck. The purse was gone.

"My handbag's been stolen!" Jirina shrieked.

"Maybe it's fallen under the seat," said Sheila, logically. Both women ducked their heads under the edge of the table.

Suddenly Sheila reappeared. "Shit!" she said, with feeling. "My purse is gone too!"

I looked around. Behind me sat a group of old ladies wearing hats smothered in artificial vegetation. At the table behind Mrs. McCavish, a group of balding gentlemen wearing plaid sportscoats and plastic name-tags dickered over the exchange rate. Could one of them, or perhaps one of the ladies in the Queen Mum hats, have taken Jirina's purse? I dismissed the idea as ridiculous.

Jirina emerged from under the table. "They're both *gone*," she wailed, distraught.

"Could you have forgotten them in the cloakroom?" suggested the former detective.

"But Mr. Boruvka—we didn't wear coats. In this weather?" said Jirina. "Anyway, I had mine when we sat down, because I took my cigarettes out of it."

Mr. Boruvka looked embarrassed and craned his neck about helplessly, searching for signs of a clue. His attention came to rest on a man wearing makeup, long pendulous earrings, and a tight-fitting dress. He was whispering something to another man in a casual, open-necked shirt; this one had a chest like a beer barrel and a walrus moustache. The man in the dress wasn't wearing a tie, but then he wasn't in trousers either, so I suppose that made it all right.

All eyes searched the floor, the seats, the window ledge. It was hopeless. The unknown thief had snatched Sheila's and Jirina's purses right out from under our noses.

It must have been the invisible man.

Mr. Boruvka roused himself from his fascinated study of the man who was confounding the dress code. The detective stood up and, looking over Jirina's head, studied the window and ledge.

"That's the second time this has happened to me here," said Jirina indignantly. "Some time ago I had supper here with Vogeltanz, and it disappeared then too."

The former detective came out of his reverie and said, "Miss Sullivan, the thing is—"

Before he could reveal what was on his mind, Sheila said, "Oh, shit!" again, only much more loudly.

"Sheila!" I objected. "Keep a grip on yourself."

Jirina shot me one of her pitying glances and Sheila retorted, "How can I? I was carrying my gun in my purse. That's all I need, especially when the police are just looking for an excuse to take away my licence."

The gun had been a gift from me. I had smuggled it in from Vienna in a silver cigar case, back in the days before skyjacking became an Olympic sport. It was a cute little silver gun with a mother-of-pearl handle, and I'd had an inscription engraved on the barrel in a jewellery store in the Mariahilferstrasse: SHEILA THE SHAMUSESS. The bore was so small it looked as though it were meant to shoot darts, not bullets. But when I'd presented her with the mini-weapon, Sheila's reaction had amazed me. Instead of being pleased, she'd been insulted. She'd considered it further proof of my incorrigible male chauvinism, as she put it, and she'd seen the tiny filigreed revolver—and she may have been right—as an attempt to make light of her work.

"Sheila," I said soothingly, "it's just a pistol for dolls."

"Dolls my eye!" she cried angrily. "It's a Colt .45, and I'm going to have to report it to the police. They'll love this."

Now it was my turn to get upset. "And where's the—"

"I gave it to Sue. She has a dog and the dog has fleas and she needed something to kill them with."

"If you'll permit me," Mr. Boruvka began again, but once more he didn't manage to finish his sentence; Jirina smacked her forehead with the flat of her hand so sharply that a wilted flower fell out of her hair.

"Here's a real mystery!" she cried. "I remember clearly how Mr. von Vogeltanz took my handbag from me that other time, and very gallantly placed it on the ledge—and before I know it, *he* comes running up with it in his hand."

"Who?" I blurted.

"If you'll permit me," Mr. Boruvka tried again.

"My ex-lover from Prague. Herman Chumac. He handed me my purse and said, 'Jirina, one of these days you're going to lose the nose off your face.' He was oozing malice. I'd just as soon slap his face as listen to that crap. But what did I do? I thanked him, of course. Fortunately, Vogeltanz doesn't understand Czech."

"Madam—" the police lieutenant began again. This time I was the one who didn't let him finish.

"When was that, Jirina?"

"Oh, not long ago. That was when Vogeltanz first offered to help me out."

Herman Chumac. I remembered how he'd been sitting in this very same restaurant with my sister, and how Heather had put a handbag on the table, rummaged through it, pulled out some photographs, and leafed through them while she and Herman had a good laugh. Then she'd sent Herman off somewhere with the handbag.

"Please—" I heard the persistent detective say, at which point his own daughter, who had come back from making her telephone call, interrupted him.

"Vogeltanz isn't at home," she announced. "And he's not in his office either, so I left him a message on his answering machine."

I stopped listening to her. They had turned the lights out in the restaurant and now, for the edification of the customers, a kind of ode to the city was coming out of the loudspeakers. In the dusk the lights of Toronto came on, and I watched the golden windows slip slowly backwards against the silhouette of the people in the restaurant. I tried to recreate that scene. Herman had reached out with his right hand towards the glittering city and produced a lady's handbag and Heather had grabbed for it. We had been sitting some distance away from Jirina and Vogeltanz.

Suddenly, the mystery became perfectly clear. The glass bubble surrounding the restaurant was nothing but a shell that didn't move at all; it was the floor and the customers that rotated. The ledge on which the handbags had been placed was fixed to this motionless outer shell. If both women had reached for their handbags precisely seventy-two minutes after they had put them down on the ledge, they would have found them in exactly the same place.

Of course, when they got home they might have discovered that someone had removed their money or a gold lighter. The same someone could have been sitting on the far side of the restaurant when he suddenly noticed heaven-sent loot coming his way.

Or—yes. Or someone might put her handbag down on the ledge, and a second someone might be waiting for it on the far side of the restaurant, waiting to remove what interested him. He might even have the gall to then return the purse to its owner, perhaps with an ironic comment about losing the nose off her face.

Someone whose own nose is shapeless?

"—the ledge stays still and the tables move," I heard the voice of the detective say. They had finally let him get a word in edgewise.

While Sheila and Jirina were gone to retrieve their purses, the detective and I were silent. A wild streak of lightning crackled across the sky like a divine bullwhip, lashing out at the city without doing any visible harm, and in the distance, over the lake, sheet lightning flickered along the horizon. I tried to remember whether I'd rolled my car window up all the way.

"Mr. Boruvka," I said, "do you know who brought Mrs. McCavish's handbag back to her?"

He looked at me. His eyes were as innocent as forget-me-nots.

"Herman Chumac," I said quietly. "He was here that evening with my sister."

In the former detective's eyes appeared what seemed to me like an unfathomable sadness.

The girls returned, happy to have recovered their property. Sheila checked at once to see if her Colt was still there. In the semi-darkness of the restaurant, its grey-black barrel gleamed a sinister gleam. Jirina checked her purse and found nothing missing.

"Mrs. McCavish," the detective said, "were you here with Vogeltanz before you were attacked in Etobicoke or was it after that?"

The owner of *Toronto Lady* pulled a stylish fan purchased in Chinatown out of her handbag and began to fan herself. The oppressive heat beyond the window was almost too much for the air conditioners to keep at bay.

"It must have been before. Otherwise I certainly would have told him about it that evening, and I didn't. I know I talk too much as a rule, but I can't—"

"And Mrs. McCavish," Mr. Boruvka interrupted, "is there any possibility that Mr. Chumac—because it was Mr. Chumac who brought your purse back to you, yes?"

"Yes, it was."

"Is there any chance he knew that you were going to dine here with Mr. von Vogeltanz that same evening? Ah," and he paused for a moment. "That is a silly question. Excuse me. If my assumption is correct—"

But Jirina was answering him. "That's possible, because the same afternoon Heather was at my place and I told her I had a supper date at the CN Tower with an Austrian aristocrat. And

Heather said, 'That's fantastic, I'm going there with Herman. Maybe we can double.' Naturally I wasn't too keen on the idea, so I told her I had some very private matters to discuss with Vogeltanz and Heather said, 'Too bad. We were supposed to go to La Chaumière but Herman just called and suggested we switch to the Tower since the visibility's so great. We might even be able to see the American side.' "

There was something not right about her story. Herman didn't strike me as a lover of touristy views.

I glanced at the detective. Our eyes met. "Mrs. McCavish," Mr. Boruvka said gloomily, "would you be so kind as to look again to see if anything is missing from your purse?"

Although she had already checked once, Jirina began another wild struggle with the clasp of her purse, finally tearing it open and pulling out something that looked like a credit card.

"Thank God!" she exclaimed.

It was a photograph of a fingerprint, encased in protective plastic. The former detective reached for it eagerly and for some time he examined it as carefully as he had the count's nose a little earlier.

"Mrs. McCavish," said the detective, "have you ever shown this to anyone else?"

Jirina replied, "Oh, my God no!" After a moment she added, "I mean, not really. Sometimes I'd pull out my credit card folder and tell people that my most important credit card of all was in there—" She stopped, then put her hand to her mouth. "Oh, I'm such a goose! I've always been too fond of blowing my own horn—"

Mr. Boruvka interrupted her. "Did you ever show that collection of cards to Mr. von Vogeltanz?"

It was dark now, and the sheet lightning on the horizon was flashing with ominous regularity. The owner of the shameless gossip tabloid blushed.

"I suppose I did, yes. Yes. When Herman brought me my purse and I checked to see if anything was missing." Jirina started fanning herself with increased energy. "Oh, my God! Am I a—"

I interrupted her.

"Jirina, did Herman know too?"

"Well—" The editor squirmed uneasily in her chair. "As a matter of fact, he did. Back in Prague. I told you I was a talkative bitch."

A gigantic flash of lightning slashed across the sky, as a crash of thunder deafened us. Below, the tiny log buildings of Old Fort York perched on their neat lawns like the toy wooden towns we used to get in our Christmas stockings. One lonely ferry glided across the sheen of the harbour, leaving a pencil-line of wake. The thunder died away into an eerie hush.

"If you will permit, Miss Sullivan," said Lieutenant Boruvka in a sepulchral voice, "I think we should all go back to your office now."

14

Evening, and Then Night

As we drove to the office a few heavy drops of rain fell on the car. The thunder seemed to be retreating, and the storm would probably amount to nothing. The flashes of lightning were far away.

The office was dark and hot. Sheila turned on the lights, walked over to her desk, and pulled open the drawer. They were still there.

The glasses. Smudged and unwashed.

The detective picked them up one by one in his handkerchief. They were still covered with sticky traces of Coca Cola bearing perfect impressions of Mr. Vogeltanz's fingerprints.

Mr. Boruvka went into the laboratory and we sat down in the waiting room; the lab was too small for everyone and Sheila's knowledge of dactyloscopy was mostly theoretical. Outside, the storm was still hanging in the balance. We were silent, each absorbed in his own thoughts. Once again, mine turned to my kid sister.

I remembered Heather's habit of smoking in the dark. She said it helped her think. In fact she was probably dreaming. But what about? Poor Heather. When she opened the door the murderer made some excuse to come into the house, followed her as far as the kitchen, and fired.

Mistaken identity.

I could still see my kid sister playing field hockey, so long ago now, with a real passion—bare knees under a plaid skirt, the uniform of St. Hilda's, where my parents had sent her to arm her against a world they knew was less than ideal. Between those bare knees and the cigarettes, between the hockey stick and the joints, time seemed to have shrunk to nothing. My little sister.

"Relax, Dad's an expert," Sue was just saying to Sheila. "I know he's not a very likely looking detective, but in Prague he really was the best. The best of them all. He would have been made head of the Homicide Division if it hadn't been for that so-called kidnapping incident."

"Why did he do it, really?" Sheila asked. "Surely it wasn't just because of the child?"

"No, it was partly because they wouldn't let Lucy and me join Mack in the States. But it was mainly because back home, his profession didn't make sense any more."

"Why not?"

"It's hard to explain—"

"Don't you start that too," said Sheila, with an irritable glance at Jirina. "Try me, I just might understand."

"Of course you might understand," said Sue, "but unless you've actually lived there— It's just that they have something like a mafia there, only it runs the whole country. If you belong to it you're absolutely safe, because it protects its own—"

"The *mafia*?" Sheila said skeptically. "Under socialism?"

The detective's daughter hesitated. She knew her boss well enough by now to realize that Sheila understood the holy terminology in its ethereal sense, purged of the cruel dross of the real world.

"I mean it's a *kind* of mafia," said Sue. "That's what everyone calls it, although the official name for it is the Communist Party.

Like the mafia, it's a law unto itself. In Dad's job he ran into it almost every day, and it started to get to him. Once, for example, a dancer was murdered and Dad had the case all sewn up, but it turned out the killer was in the mafia—so instead of sending him to jail they packed him off to an embassy post in Ghana. Another time—"

"Are the police on the take, the way they are in the States?"

"No, not exactly. The police are just extremely well paid, better than most people, and have all kinds of bonuses and privileges. They obey orders. Occasionally one faction of the mafia—I mean the Party—uses the police to get rid of another which is losing ground. Once they even hanged twelve of them, all at once—"

I looked at Sue and suddenly I had the strangest feeling. My God, I thought, has this bloody case turned me into a poet rather than a hardboiled detective? In Sheila's pale cheeks I seemed to glimpse a lovely countryside of rolling fields and maple woodlots shrouded in morning mist, but in the tanned cheeks of Sue McLaughlin, that girl from a far-off country, I sensed wild mountains capped with thunderheads, a bleak landscape of dried-up lakes and rivers that ran no more. And her animated voice could create an instant intimacy suspended above all this, like a comic counterpoint to her sadness. Even her garrulousness seemed natural, an expression not of a young woman's inclination to chatter, but of a rich and formless treasury of tall tales and epic romance.

"...until Father found the skull. The killer got fifteen years, but two years later he was let off for good behaviour. That was just after the invasion. He was a real cutthroat, but I guess they...."

"It *is* just like the States!" my girl exclaimed. "The poor murderers get life and the ones with money and connections get...." Sheila looked as though she'd made a great discovery. "It's exactly the same!" she exclaimed again.

Sue looked at her for a moment, and then said, "Sheila, do you enjoy your work?"

"Enjoy my work? Why—of course I do. What's that got to do with anything?"

"What do you like about it?"

"I like the idea of being able to help women—people, that is— who need a little justice and might not necessarily get it from the police."

"So you still believe justice is possible?"

"Well, yes—but not all the time. When—"

"But enough that it makes your job worth while?"

"Yes."

"Then it's not exactly the same. You still believe in justice. My father no longer could. And he was one of the last to give up hope, believe me."

"Was he a socialist?"

"I suppose he still is, bless him. He'll never get over that as long as he lives. He's a first-class detective but basically he's a little bit of a fool. A very kind-hearted old fool." She spoke with affection.

The man they were talking about came into the waiting room from the lab, looking like misery personified.

Before the detective could speak, the telephone rang. It was Bill Kendrick. I handed the receiver to Sheila. From her reactions, I gathered that the confidential information he was slipping her was particularly confidential this time.

Sheila hung up, collapsed on a chair, and uttered a polite phrase that sounded completely sincere. "I could sure do with a drink."

"Me too," said Jirina, who up till then had been keeping unusually quiet. She was probably still in shock over what her "blowing of her own horn" had caused—and might yet cause.

I went into Sheila's inner office and came back with two glasses. In a single gulp, Sheila drained more than half a double Marlowe. Then she peered at the detective, who was still standing in the doorway looking like a man whose father had just bequeathed the family fortune to his cats.

"Trcka wasn't a count at all," said Sheila, addressing me in particular. "His real name was Jan something-or-other and Interpol have been looking for him since 1968. They found this out when they did a routine check on his fingerprints today. He's been in Canada off and on since 1969, but since 1968 he's been wanted by the Czech police for the murder of his ex-wife. It seems he divorced her but he couldn't get her to move out of his apartment, so he killed her. I can hardly believe that, but that's what Bill said."

"She probably had nowhere else to live," said Jirina drily.

The detective uttered a hollow sound. We all turned to look at him.

"I...that picture," he said. "I had the feeling I'd seen him somewhere before. Back then he had a beard and light hair. He also had rotten teeth."

Mr. Boruvka was holding the glass and Jirina's card in his hand. Sheila looked at him questioningly. His expression became sad. "They don't match," he said, as though he were announcing the death of his best friend.

Sheila got up energetically. "I'm going to call Bill and ask him to get Trcka's fingerprints for us."

"I'm afraid that would be—" Boruvka began, then stopped because Sheila had already picked up the phone and dialled. "—of no use," he said, more or less to himself.

But my girl was already dictating her request to the love-smitten detective at the other end of the line. She ended her conversation with an impatient, "Oh, don't worry, nobody will know. I'm alone here."

"There's still Herman," I said when she had finished. "What about his fingerprints?"

Sheila thought. A furrow appeared between her eyebrows. "I have no right to take them, unless Bill Kendrick—"

"There's no need for that." I smiled at her and took the cigar case out of my pocket. "Of course, it's going to be covered with my own prints," I said, handing it to the detective, "but perhaps you'll find something." I told him about the mistake in the Old English Pub.

Oddly enough, Mr. Boruvka didn't seem enthusiastic about the idea, but all he said was "I don't know if it will do any good."

"But Herman must be mixed up in this somehow," I said. "He was seen wandering around the scene of the crime. He was in the Savoy when Trcka died, and he had his mitts on Jirina's handbag at the CN Tower."

"But don't forget," said Mr. Boruvka timidly, "that Mrs. McCavish was mugged *after* she had supper there with von Vogeltanz."

"But what does that prove?" I asked.

"It doesn't prove anything," replied Mr. Boruvka, "but it suggests—" He looked closely at the well-handled cigar case. "Well, just to be sure, I'll compare it, but I don't think it will tell us anything." And he turned and walked back into the lab.

I looked at Sheila, who telegraphed exasperation with her eyes. Herman? Trcka? Vogeltanz? Krsic? All or none of the above? It was all so complicated that I thought back, almost wistfully, to my original suspicions of Harrison Morrison. But if he was involved, then all these other events were coincidences— and such coincidences don't happen, even in the worst Victorian melodramas.

I went into Sheila's inner office and brought the bottle back into the waiting room. Even the detective's daughter went for a double Marlowe this time. With my second glass of whisky that evening, I walked over to the window. The eighteenth floor afforded a beautiful view of night-time Toronto. The mist had been blown away by the storm and the black thunderhead was now skewered on the upper half of the CN Tower. The people in the restaurant would no longer be able to see the city. Lightning was flickering back and forth among the clouds. The heat seemed to have reached the boiling point.

A door squeaked. I turned around. The mournful detective appeared in the lab door and the expression on his face answered all our unspoken questions. He walked over to Jirina and handed her the piece of plastic.

"Unfortunately they don't match," he said in his funereal voice. "But I would say it's inconclusive."

I saw him staring at my glass. He was too timid to ask for a drink, but his blue eyes were eloquent enough. I offered him a double Marlowe, which he accepted gratefully. Then he went on, "Of course, if my hypothesis should prove correct it won't be of any use to us anyway."

"What hypothesis?" I said, perhaps too abruptly. The detective had an annoying habit of assuming we understood what he was thinking. He looked at me apologetically and then turned to the owner of *Toronto Lady*. Before he could answer my question, however, Jirina jumped to her feet and exclaimed: "I've been robbed! That's not my card! This one has rounded corners, and mine was squared! That's not the same fingerprint at all!"

My mind was racing. As soon as two ideas connected and began to make sense, a third would come along and slice through them like a razor. A lot of people knew about the card. Herman had had a good chance to examine it when he carried Jirina's purse back to her through the revolving restaurant. And it would have been a simple matter for the night-time mugger to exchange a bogus print for the real one. So far, so good. But was any of this probable? Well, why not? And anyway, why should it have to be probable?

Someone rang the buzzer. Bill Kendrick? "You wait here and be quiet," Sheila admonished us, and she left the room and closed the door behind her. Naturally, Kendrick wouldn't want witnesses to his breach of confidence. I went to the door, opened it slightly, and peeked out. It was Kendrick, all right. He certainly hadn't wasted any time getting here; probably used the siren. He was a tall and somewhat beefy plainclothes detective, with a regulation moustache and those standard-issue shoes that always give them away. I felt a twitch of jealousy, for although I was certain I could beat him on the squash courts, no doubt there were other fields of physical endeavour where his kind of dogged persistence would excel. For a moment I thought of writing his boss an anonymous letter about his unethical collaboration, but I instantly felt ashamed; the only decent way to deal with a rivalry is openly. I probably should have hit him, as Harrison had done to Krsic last night in Kitchener. But Kendrick didn't look like the kind of person who was used to turning the other cheek. Gloomily I watched as the love-struck detective followed Sheila into her office. They remained there an unnecessarily long time, considering that all he had to do was give her an envelope. But eventually she managed to get rid of him. We heard the office door closing, and Sheila came back and gave the envelope to Mr. Boruvka. For a third time he vanished into the laboratory, his face a picture of unhappiness.

A long time went by. I had to go into Sheila's office for another bottle. As I stared down at the city again I noticed to my bemusement that all the office towers had double windows, two golden rectangles of light overlapping each other, like a 3-D photograph seen without the glasses.

"I don't think I feel very well," I heard Sue say. "I'm not used to drinking like this."

Once, not so long ago, my kid sister wasn't used to drinking either. When was it she first came home drunk? Someone brought her back, I heard the crunch of a car stopping suddenly under the window, and a few moments later a door slammed and the car roared off. Her escort had merely leaned her against the door frame, rung the bell, and cleared off. I opened the front door and Heather collapsed into my arms, and I smelled the familiar sickly sweetness of bourbon on her breath. In a fury of moral indignation I began berating her, though she was all but unconscious—and I'd been known to come home in a similar state myself. Finally my father came out of his bedroom and said, "Leave her alone, Neil, I'll talk to her in the morning," and we half led, half carried her to her room, the one with the photos of Bonnie Prince Charles in his bachelor days, with her high-school trophies and school pennants. No matter how much at odds she was with Father or the world, she'd always come back home when the bloom had worn off a new boyfriend, back to this ample house where the traditions of the Donbys, such as they are, were still strong enough to blot the world out for a while. I knew how she felt, for I would come home too for the very same reasons, and spend the night under the old family roof. And when we'd put her to bed, I'd return to my room and try, unsuccessfully, to sleep. Later that night I'd hear familiar sounds coming from the bathroom, the kind they never tell you about in television ads, the sounds of a digestive system retching itself clean once more.

I took another drink from my glass. The windows of the city were now tripled as they glowed into the tropical night and illuminated the low ceiling of black cloud. The door squeaked.

"Nothing?" I heard Sheila's anxious voice say. I turned around, steadying myself against the window-frame. The old detective's face was like a mask from a Greek tragedy, but what he said was at odds with his expression of bottomless sadness.

"This time the prints match."

"Trcka!" shrieked Jirina.

So it had been the count. It hardly seemed surprising—he'd already murdered his wife just to get more floor-space. I took another drink and grabbed the window-frame for support.

"It proves only one thing," said the sepulchral voice. "And, if you'll permit me, we don't need proof of that."

"What do you mean, we don't need proof?" Sheila almost shouted.

"Miss Sullivan," said Lieutenant Boruvka, with a patient politeness that seemed out of place, "we already know that someone switched the fingerprints. This merely confirms it."

"How?" gasped Jirina.

The detective turned his basset-hound eyes on her. "The switching of the fingerprints proves one thing: your father's murderer is still alive, and afraid he'll be found out. The fact that the fingerprints match is also a clue."

"How?" I blurted.

"I think the murderer has gone too far. These fingerprints point too conspicuously to someone who was involved with your sister. But since we know about the switch, we know that the man who switched them knew a lot about Trcka. So most probably the murderer is either—"

"Vogeltanz!" said Sue.

"Or Herman Chumac," I said.

"Or both," added Sue.

Both?

Of course! Vogeltanz knew Jirina would be out—why else would he spend the evening in the Old English Pub? His secretary did *not* forget to tell him.

On the other hand, Herman knew Heather....

Was Sheila right, after all?

The detective's voice descended to a tone appropriate to the eighth circle of hell. "I'm afraid it may have been both of them. But I don't know how we're going to prove anything now that the original fingerprints are gone."

And with that, the owner of *Toronto Lady* uttered a whoop of delight.

We all turned to stare at her.

"I may be a goose, but I'm not *that* stupid. I have the originals in a safety deposit box. This—" she waved the switched card "—I mean the one this was switched for—had 'copy' pencilled on the back."

Lieutenant Boruvka, who was just taking a sip of whisky, began to choke.

"Why didn't you say—"

"Oh shit!" mumbled the editor and blushed. "I guess I *am* a goose, after all."

15

You Can't Make an Omelette...

That night the storm finally broke. The stifling heat became unbearable and then everything exploded in a savage burst of thunder and lightning that crackled among the towers of the city and melted lightning rods.

I slept at Sheila's place. Actually, I didn't sleep, nor did Sheila. She merely lay there with her eyes squeezed shut, trying to imagine that she wasn't afraid. I'd seen her like this before. She had lost both her parents, and almost died herself, in just such a vicious storm on Lake Ontario. It was back in the days when I first knew her. She had gone sailing on Lake Ontario with her parents—it was one of her rare attempts to reach across the ideological rift that had come between them—and violent winds suddenly blew up from the American side of the lake, catching the yacht halfway between Toronto and Rochester. Clouds seething with electricity scudded low over the waves and the yacht began to toss about. As Mr. Sullivan was battling to reef in the mainsail, a bolt of lightning like the archangel's sword struck the mast, the gasoline tank in the hold exploded, and in a fraction of a second Sheila became an orphan and an heiress. She was at the helm when it happened and the explosion tossed her into the water and away from the burning wreck. She was rescued several hours later by the harbour police.

And so she was left with a trauma and her father's fortune. The fortune was safe—luckily it was tied up in various investments—but Sheila herself was in pretty bad shape. She took her parents' death unexpectedly badly, considering that the best thing I'd ever heard her say about them when they were alive was that they were "petty bourgeois capitalist exploiters of the toiling masses".

Later Sheila became a very sensitive meteorologist. Whenever a storm caught us somewhere together, I watched with great sympathy as she tried to behave like Modesty Blaise; with each flash of lightning I knew she was counting the seconds before the thunder came rolling over us.

That night it was impossible to count. Sheets of water assaulted the rooftops and lashed the pavement, and whenever the lightning cracked, the explosion was on us instantly, like gigantic shelves of slate splitting in two.

In all the commotion, I suddenly remembered that Jirina was at home alone in her empty house. Both Sheila and Sue had offered to move in with her until the question of the murder was settled, and the detective, in his gloomy voice, had urged her to accept the offer, but the owner of *Toronto Lady* wouldn't hear of it. "I'm not afraid," she said resolutely. "Just let him try something. I'm ready for him." And she hefted the Colt Sheila had given her. I noticed with horror that the safety catch was off.

My premonition of danger, which sat like a constriction in my throat, was much like the one I had had the day before—the one that had turned out to be not entirely unfounded. As the lightning sizzled over Sheila's bungalow, which was outfitted with a forest of sophisticated lightning rods, I thought of Jirina sleeping less than a mile from us, guarded only by her non-violent tomcat, while governments, or at least agents of foreign powers, plotted against her life.

Towards morning the storm finally subsided and I fell asleep. When I awoke the sun was already high in the sky, the air was fresh, and Sheila was sleeping beside me like a corpse. The telephone rang. I looked at my watch; it was past eleven. Somewhat apprehensively, I answered the phone. It was Sue, calling to say there were some people waiting to see us at the office.

We arrived at the office before twelve, bringing with us three bottles of rye that we'd bought on the way. Although it was rather early to be drinking, Sue began to pour drinks into sparkling clean glasses, and not even Vogeltanz refused. After all, it was almost lunch time, and he could consider the drink an aperitif.

Vogeltanz's glass bore the etched symbol of Scorpio, and he was turning it over thoughtfully in his long, elegant fingers. Beside him, just as thoughtfully, Herman Chumac was contemplating a glass which had a stylized image of Libra on it. Nikola Krsic, whose glass carried a Taurus, was behaving in exactly the same way, and I was drinking from a Virgo, while Sheila had a Capricorn and Sue, though she was on duty, was sipping modestly from a Gemini.

The glasses had been my idea. When I learned from Sue that what amounted to a general assembly of prime suspects was waiting for us in the office, I bought them at a discount store on the way. Now, looking from glass to glass, I tried to remember which sign of the zodiac belonged to which suspect.

Vogeltanz's secretary had finally managed to pass a message on to her boss, and Sue had telephoned Herman late the night before. Krsic had shown up unexpectedly on his own, not, he said, for any particular reason; he was merely curious to know what we'd discovered, because he couldn't get my sister's tragic fate out of his mind.

So they sat there in a row, and for some reason they reminded me of those three monkeys that used to be popular as bookends or paperweights, one covering his eyes, the second his ears, and the third his mouth.

So far nothing we had discovered had helped us. Mr. von Vogeltanz had carefully studied Trcka's picture and had said that he was *almost* certain that the count and Bignose were *not* the same person.

"The nose," he said, sipping his rye and holding the photograph at various distances from his monocle, "*ja, die Nase stimmt*. But otherwise? It was the eyes. *Die Augen*," and he closed his own eyes and called up the spirit of the past. "That nose could be it, but the chap in question almost certainly had black eyes. This chap," and here he opened his eyes wide, "has grey eyes, at least if you can believe the colours in this photo."

He removed the monocle from his blue right eye.

"Also, he seems too young to me," he went on. "How old is he now? Fifty?"

"Forty-seven," said Sheila. We had learned Trcka's exact age from Sheila's admirer in Homicide.

He shook his head. "He would have been a child in 1942."

I lifted my glass to take a sip but it was empty; we must have been drinking like sailors. Sheila was just finishing her drink, and so was Mr. Vogeltanz. It was time for a refill. Sue collected the glasses and took them into Sheila's office to refill them with ice. Exactly according to my instructions, she came back with an identical set etched with the signs of the zodiac. The used glasses remained behind, to await the detective's arrival when his shift finished in the early afternoon.

With them was a piece of paper with a list of who had been drinking from which glass, so we wouldn't get them mixed up.

Mr. Krsic suddenly broke into the pause that had prevailed while the new drinks were being served. "What's going on here?" he asked in a threatening voice. "Who's this Bignose character, anyway? And who exactly is this guy here supposed to recognize?" And his black eyes glowered at the monocle.

"Mr. Krsic, that has nothing to do with what really interests us here," said the man with the monocle. His voice was soothing. *"Das ist eine alte Geschichte."*

"I'll bet it's an old *war* story," said Krsic even more darkly. "You said it was in 1942, didn't you?"

"That's right. That's why this business has nothing to do with the unfortunate death of Miss Donby. What we were talking about just now is more or less a private matter, of interest only to the editor of—"

"And who's this editor you're talking about?" Krsic pressed.

"Mrs. Jirina McCavish, editor of *Toronto Lady*."

"Never heard of her," roared Krsic. "What the hell is going on here, anyway? I thought you people were looking into Heather's death. Why are you going on about some newspaper editor? And what's the war got to do with anything?"

"I'm afraid I'm not permitted to speak about Mrs. McCavish," said the monocle. "Of course, if Miss Sullivan would—"

"That really doesn't belong here," Herman butted into the conversation. "It has nothing to do with Heather's—with Miss Donby's—death. Jirina has the fingerprints of a former Gestapo agent with a large nose who—"

His voice died as Krsic looked him up and down. The Balkanite put all the power of his eyes into it, and examined Herman from head to toe very slowly, finally concentrating on his olfactory organ. Then he said with heavy irony, "And speaking of noses, whatever happened to *yours*?"

Naturally we all turned our attention to Herman. Surrounded by the haggard and careworn features of his face, his schnozz no longer seemed such an anomaly.

But there was still something not right about that nose.

"Did you fight with the resistance too?" continued Krsic threateningly. "And how old were you in 1942?"

"Twenty-two," Herman shot back. Either he was good at mental arithmetic or he had his answer prepared. "Listen, you surely don't think—" and Herman turned red, as though he were about to have a stroke.

"All I'm saying is, don't try to tell us you were born with a crushed banana like that."

He had defined the shape of Herman's nose exactly.

"I used to box when I was a kid," said Herman. "I tried surgery, but they botched it several times and they never did manage to get it right. Socialist medicine. And—" Herman looked around. It occurred to me that at that moment he did resemble a boxer—on the ropes.

"And anyway," he said, in an insulted tone, "Jirina has the fingerprints of this Bignose character. Here!" And he stretched out his hands with the palms turned upwards, almost in supplication, towards Krsic. Then he realized how inappropriate this was, and held them out to Sheila. "Here! Take my fingerprints! Compare them, if you don't believe me!"

A tense silence followed, and in that silence Mr. von Vogeltanz took a drink and then looked carefully at the zodiacal sign on his glass. Sue had made a mistake. On his fresh glass there was not a Scorpio, but a Capricorn. Mr. von Vogeltanz put on his monocle and studied the mythic beast. Then he put the glass down on the coffee table.

"How is it that *you* know about Mrs. McCavish's fingerprints, *Herr* Chumac?" he asked in a voice like a dagger.

Herman turned even redder and began to sputter. "I—she used to—that is, we used to be good friends, in Prague. She—she told me about it, and I happen to know that she carries them around with her."

"Did she ever compare them with your prints?" asked Sheila.

"No! Why should she have? That's absurd. Why, it's—" And again he held his hands out to Sheila like a sleepwalker. "Compare them yourself."

"Good idea!" thundered Nikola Krsic and a second pair of hands was presented for inspection by the proprietress of the Watchful Sisters. I wondered if they would have offered their hands so willingly had they known that the card removed from Jirina's handbag was only a copy, and that the original was still safe.

"The card Mrs. McCavish carried around in her purse could easily have been switched by someone," said Sheila coolly. "Not long ago she had her purse snatched—"

"Ah, so the card is missing, is it?" asked von Vogeltanz with interest.

"No, they only took some money and a manuscript. They threw the handbag away. Mrs. McCavish found it and the card was still there."

Von Vogeltanz raised his eyebrows. "So the thieves—that is, if they weren't just ordinary muggers—had time to switch the fingerprints on her. Of course, to succeed in their scheme they would have to know in advance what this card looked like."

"So they would," said Sheila. "But do you recall what happened to her purse when she was having supper with you in the CN Tower? That was just a few days before the mugging."

The monocle hid one half of von Vogeltanz's reaction. "*Ach ja, da haben Sie Recht*," he laughed. "She lost it somewhere. Fortunately—" and he paused significantly, "fortunately Mr. Chumac here found it for her, since he was, by chance, dining in the same restaurant."

Herman threw him an unfriendly glance. "But that handbag—I was sitting on the other side of the restaurant all the time."

"With my sister," I said harshly.

Herman literally twitched. He clearly did not know which implication to defend himself against first—theft or murder. But then he regained his composure. "The handbag came to us along the ledge. It travelled halfway around the restaurant. Anyone could have—"

149

"Anyone who was interested in its contents—" said Sheila icily.

"Interested?" Herman groaned. "Look, I insist that you take my fingerprints."

For the third time he held his hands out towards Sheila, as though he were trying to levitate. This time, however, he pulled them back rapidly. "But that means—" and an expression crossed his face that I could not interpret—was it relief? "If someone switched that card on Jirina, then the prints can't prove—"

He didn't finish what he was saying.

With a malice that surprised me, Krsic said, "What if someone slipped the lady a card with *your* fingerprints on it?"

"Why mine? How could they get them?"

"Easily," replied Krsic. "You're a drinker, right? There must be glasses everywhere that you've taken a drink from. Here, for instance," and he pointed to the mythological bestiary. "See? There's a different animal on each glass. There's a fish on mine. All you have to do is remember who had what, and when we're gone Miss Private Detective here," and he nodded towards Sheila, "can take them into her Devil's Kitchen and—surprise, surprise!"

From the corner of my eye, I saw Mr. von Vogeltanz grin. He took his glass from the table and very deliberately pressed his thumb against the glass. Then he looked contentedly at the result through his monocle.

"If the card was switched," said Herman coldly, "and my prints are on it, it will prove the real killer was trying to lay the blame on an inno—"

Von Vogeltanz interrupted him. "But you'd have to prove they *were* switched. Calm down!"

Herman failed to see the difficulty of making such a proof and his confidence returned. "If they weren't, then I've got nothing to worry about. Take my fingerprints," and he held his hands out to Sheila once more. But Krsic dashed his hopes.

"And if Miss Private Detective here proves they weren't switched, and your prints are on them—"

With his arms comically outstretched, Herman made a quick left turn, military style.

"—then you'll be in the soup."

A nasty grin appeared on Herman's face. "If Miss Private Detective proves they weren't switched, then I'm out of any soup you may think I'm in."

Sheila said coldly—and I was beginning to feel that she was, after all, becoming a real detective:

"There's not just *one* soup in the case. You dated Heather. You were seen prowling around Jirina's house on the night of the murder. And you are known to have treated Heather brutally, in the most despicable male chauvinist fashion."

Cracks appeared in Herman's calm demeanour.

"Well—yes—I did carry on disgracefully. I'm terribly sorry about that. But I didn't...."

"I can relieve you of some of your worries," I said, when Herman didn't seem to be able to finish his sentence.

"What worries?" barked Krsic.

"That you won't be able to clear yourself of the—let's call it the fingerprint suspicion."

"How?"

For a moment I looked from one to the other. Krsic was bristling with anger, Herman was still trembling slightly, and von Vogeltanz was looking at me with intelligent eyes behind which a cool brain was working.

"I see no other possibility," he said almost sweetly, "of clearing us—as you put it—or, perhaps, of clearing *two* of us?—than this: there must be another copy of the original prints somewhere. Am I right?"

I rewarded him with a glowing smile. "Precisely."

"Where?" gasped Herman.

I looked at my watch and blew a mouthful of smoke towards the ceiling. It was almost one o'clock. "I don't know. But if you can wait here until half past two, you'll have a chance to see them yourselves."

I realized, suddenly, that I had said too much. I was behaving almost like Jirina. All three suspects were sitting here, drawing conclusions from the information I had so casually offered them, and it would hardly require a Sherlock Holmes to figure out the answers.

"Jirina!" Herman gasped. "She had them at home somewhere and now—she's on her way here with them!" He fell back in his chair.

"I've had enough of this garbage," said Krsic, getting up from his chair and turning towards the door.

I rose to block him and his black eyes bored pure hatred into mine. "Get out of my way."

Just when an act of physical violence seemed the only possible outcome, a calm voice said from behind me, "Let him go, Mr. Donby."

Krsic turned around. Von Vogeltanz was tapping a cigarette butt out of his silver holder and sticking his monocle into his pocket. "This is a civilized country," he said with a smile. "The police are sufficiently well equipped to track down a man with—*wie soll ich's sagen*—Mr. Krsic's remarkable distinguishing features. So let him go. Even if the fingerprints do not match, running away is generally considered the equivalent of an admission of guilt."

Krsic darkened. He stepped back from the door. "Who says I'm running away? I'm just fed up with the whole goddamned business. It's got nothing to do with me. But I'm not so sure that applies to everyone in this mess." He stabbed the Austrian with a black look. "I'm not so sure at all."

Mr. von Vogeltanz held his hand out to him. "*Ein Moment, bitte*. What if you were to go with me? Let me invite you to lunch. The thing is—" and he glanced at his wristwatch, "this is most awkward, but I regret to say I have an extremely important business lunch at the Graf Bobby, and I should have been there already." He turned to address Nikola Krsic again. "But my meeting, with a Mr. Biener, will be brief. Then we can sit down and discuss—*so gesagt*—matters of common interest. Or perhaps of the past?" He looked at Nikola in an almost kindly fashion. "May I make a telephone call, Miss Sullivan?"

Sheila was clearly exhausted by the dramatic course of events. She merely nodded and reached for the bottle of rye, but it was empty. Sue stood up, picked up the ice bucket, and went into Sheila's office for another one.

Acting on a sudden impulse, I got up and followed her. In the next room Sue started unscrewing the metal cap of another bottle. "God, I wish Dad were here," she whispered. "I'm completely baffled by all this, aren't you?"

I couldn't bring myself to admit that I felt pretty much the same way. I merely put my finger to my lips, lifted the receiver, and heard a telephone ringing. "Graf Bobby Café, may I help you?" someone said on the other end. Mr. von Vogeltanz asked if he could speak to a Mr. Biener. A few moments later someone with a German accent picked up the phone and the aristocratic businessman, with an elegant apology, asked him to be patient for just a while longer, explaining that he had been held up by an important meeting but was now on his way. Then he hung up. Sue looked at me questioningly.

"Who was he talking to?"

"Someone called Biener," I shrugged.

"Vogeltanz is a sharpie," said Sue. "And I don't like his face. What time is it?"

I looked at my watch. "It's past one."

"Dad's shift is almost over. Oh, I wish he were here now." She walked over to the liquor cabinet and began to chip ice into the ice bucket.

I went back to the waiting room. Herman was just drinking the last drops of melted ice from the bottom of his glass. A golden crab glistened on the side of it. Krsic was hovering indecisively by his chair and Mr. von Vogeltanz was talking to him. What he was saying was intended for Sheila.

"Not only will we be able to clear certain things up, Mr. Krsic, but my invitation has a practical purpose as well: we shall each ensure that the other does not run away, and my partner, Mr. Biener, will keep an eye on both of us." He took Krsic by the wrist and then turned to Sheila. "May we, Miss Sullivan?"

Sheila nodded foolishly, as if in a trance; I wondered just how much rye she had downed. Krsic glowered at the Austrian aristocrat and then assented. Von Vogeltanz hooked his arm under Krsic's and led him to the door, as though they were the best of friends.

Common sense told me to stop them, to keep them there until Mr. Boruvka arrived. I looked at Sheila. She was as pale as death, and teetering. Instead of barring the two men, I stepped up to her and took her by the arm, allowing both suspects to walk out of the office, arm in arm.

As the door closed behind them, the detective's daughter came back with the bottle and the ice and immediately saw what had happened. "My God!" she cried. "You let them go?"

Sheila's colour rapidly returned and went to the opposite extreme. "But it's logical," she said uncertainly. "Whoever runs away—if either one does—will have more or less confessed."

"To what?" cried Sue.

She was right. To what?

"To—" Sheila's cornflower-blue eyes appealed to me for help. I was moved by the mute look of genuine helplessness in them. "To—" she repeated weakly, and then she pulled her arm away from mine. "Oh, shit!"

She reached for her glass, the one with the sign of Capricorn on it, and poured herself a stiff drink. Then she belted it down like a lumberjack. I had never seen her do that before.

A crazy thought crossed my mind. We'd assumed that the one person beyond suspicion was the editor of *Toronto Lady*.

But was she?

Had we checked to see what time she had left for Kitchener that day? Was there anyone who could vouch for her alibi? My sister had died in her home, and she had been having an affair with the editor's former lover—although, again, who could say how "former" he really was?

"Shit!" I exclaimed, and took a swig straight from the bottle myself.

The four-letter word echoed into a tomb-like silence.

In that silence, a figure suddenly streaked past me. Before I could recover my senses, Herman had knocked Sue backwards over the coffee table, so that she bumped her head on the corner of a chair, and had dashed out of the office with a mad look in his eyes.

I had no strength in me any more to run after him.

That left us with a bottle of whisky in the desk drawer and a few sticky glasses as our only remaining connection to Phil Marlowe.

Someone knocked.

"Come in!" I shouted, ashamed and angry.

The door opened and the former detective stood there. His melancholy eyes looked around the room and then stopped at his daughter, who was just gathering herself up from the floor and shaking her head woozily.

"Am I interrupting something?" he said.

"Oh Dad," cried his daughter. "How can you ask such dumb questions?"

Mr. Boruvka looked embarrassed. "Someone just jumped into one elevator as I was getting out of the other," he said. "I had the impression—"

"That was Herman. Oh Dad, we let them all get away!"

"Who?"

"Vogeltanz, Herman, Krsic—"

He interrupted her abruptly. "Has Mrs. McCavish been here already?"

"She was supposed to come at half past two."

Mr. Boruvka pulled out a pocket watch. It looked a little odd, and when I got a closer look I saw that instead of normal watch hands it had two tiny arms ending in white gloves. Mr. Boruvka had a genuine Mickey Mouse pocket watch. I looked at my own watch. It said half past one.

"Dad," said Sue guiltily. I began to feel redundant. I glanced out of the corner of my eye, and saw that Sheila the Shamusess had surrendered unconditionally to the bottle. "Dad," Sue said, "they know all about those—about the other fingerprints."

The former detective moved to the telephone with a swiftness that was remarkable for someone of his age. He dialled a number, said "Hello," and babbled something in what must have been Czech. Then he stopped and tried to say something in English, but he couldn't seem to get it out. He turned to me and held out the receiver. "Could you take it, please?"

"Who are you calling?"

"Mrs. McCavish. But an Englishman answered it."

I almost ripped the receiver out of his hands.

"Hello?"

"Hello?" said a voice that sounded oddly familiar.

"Who is this?"

"Who is *this*?"

"Is this Mrs. McCavish's residence?" I asked.

"Yes."

"Could I speak to her, please?"

"She's just stepped out for cigarettes."

Where had I heard that voice before? I froze.

"*Harrison?*" I whispered.

"Yes?" said the voice.

"Harrison! What the hell are you doing at Jirina's?"

"Is that you, Neil?"

Instead of answering, I shouted again, "What the hell are you doing there?"

"Take it easy," Harrison said, and I could hear him laughing. "As far as I can tell, I'm supposed to be some kind of bodyguard."

"Bodyguard?"

"Mrs. McCavish is supposed to be bringing this super-important document to your fiancée-to-be's office, and she got frightened. So she called me. You people have got her pretty terrified. Whose idea was it to give her a gun she doesn't know how to use?"

"Has anything happened?" I remembered how awkwardly Jirina had played with the weapon the night before.

"No, but—"

"Why didn't she call me?"

Harrison laughed. "She did but you were out."

"Why didn't she call Sheila's office!"

"Ask her. My impression is that she played the big hero in front of you all yesterday and then everything kind of hit her last night when she was alone. In any case—"

"Stay with her!" I cut in. "She *is* in danger. There's a fellow on his way over there now—God, maybe two or three of them—"

"Son of a bitch," said Harrison.

"And one of them—maybe all of them, for all I know—is probably armed."

"Wonderful."

"Harrison, you know how to use a pistol, don't you?"

"I sure do," said Harrison, and he laughed again. "But look, when I got here she told me the gun didn't work, said she'd tried shooting it in the garden this morning and nothing happened when she pulled the trigger."

"Sounds like she had the safety on."

Harrison chuckled. "No, she had it off, but—" His laughter was beginning to get on my nerves. "I'll give you three guesses what the matter was, and the first two don't count."

"Come on, Harrison, this is serious."

"To make a long story short," said Harrison calmly, "it wasn't loaded. And there's not a bullet in the house."

"Have you got a rod with you?"

"A *rod*? Hey Neil, what's this Mickey Spillane stuff? I don't own a handgun. I only have my competition shotguns." He was being infuriatingly calm, and he added, "I can hardly carry them around with me."

"Harrison," I said, gritting my teeth, "whatever you do, don't leave her. Get yourself a knife or a club or *something*."

"Do you seriously think there's a murderer on his way over?"

"At least two."

"Great. At last I can see whether all those karate courses I took were worth the money. Are you coming too?"

"Yes. Stay right where you are. I'll be there in—ten minutes."

"See you later," he replied with incomprehensible calm and hung up.

Was he telling the truth? Had Jirina really invited him?

I didn't have much time to think about it.

"I have to get to Jirina's as fast as I can," I yelled at the detective. "Harrison Morrison is with her." I turned to Sheila. "That pistol of yours—you forgot to load it."

This accusation snapped Sheila out of her lethargy. "I did not," she protested. "It's always loaded."

"Harrison claims it wasn't."

"Then someone must have fired it." And Sheila once more turned the colour of clinical death.

Who was telling the truth? But there was no time to think about it now.

"Someone must remain here," I heard the detective say. "Zuzanka, you stay here with Miss Sullivan. Lock the door, and keep it locked."

I looked at the head shamusess. She was a clear candidate for remaining behind. Sue was just putting a cold compress on her forehead, filled with ice cubes from the zodiac glasses.

"Let's go, Mr. Donby," the detective said. When I turned around he was already on his way out the door and it was all I could do to catch up with him as he ran for the elevators. He stood there with his finger on the button. The sadness or whatever it was in his expression almost knocked me out.

"He didn't know your sister would be there that evening, Mr. Donby," he said. "His secretary is unreliable. She forgets to pass on messages. It was Mrs. McCavish he was after."

What was he talking about? *Who* was he talking about? The illuminated numbers above the elevator door blinked on and off. The elevator was approaching. Then I realized who he meant.

"But he knew my sister!"

"The murderer didn't," said Lieutenant Boruvka. "And that cost your sister her life."

16

...Without Breaking Eggs

The elevator doors opened and we jumped in. And we both recoiled in shock.

In the corner of the elevator, on the floor, lay Nikola Krsic. Fresh blood was oozing from a gash on his head. He had been struck with something—something hard.

The door slid closed behind us.

"They were supposed to keep an eye on each other," I said.

Lieutenant Boruvka coolly pushed the ground-floor button. I looked at the former partisan, or whatever he was. The detective bent over him once more and took his wrist. Then he looked at me with that deep sadness in his gentle eyes.

"He's not dead—not yet. But...." He touched Krsic's skull gingerly. "I think his head is broken. It looks like a blow from a gun butt. He was afraid to shoot him, you see, in case you heard."

Had the partisan fought his last battle?

And what had the battle been about?

The elevator came to a halt and the door slid open. An old man with a little dog was just getting into the other car. The dog sniffed, ran to the end of his leash, and began to bark furiously at our elevator. "Quiet, Nero," the man scolded him, dragging him into the elevator on his leash. The doors slid shut on the yapping dog. And on the ominously silent Nikola.

Boruvka made a quick call to his daughter in the office upstairs and then we rushed out to my car. The transit strike had started, and with the subway shut down traffic was terrible—I ran into a real bottleneck at the foot of Avenue Road. Fortunately an ambulance passed me on Queen's Park Crescent, and I managed to slip into its wake. We ran the lights all the way to Princess Margaret Hospital, and when the ambulance finally squealed into the hospital gates we were only a couple of blocks from Sackville Street. Even so, I had to slow down. The rye was working against the adrenaline, and even though Wellesley straightens out as you pass the hospital, I felt as though I were hurtling down a bobsled run. I gripped the wheel for dear life.

It was a beautiful, fresh, late-summer day. The overnight storm had drawn all the humidity out of the air and the sunshine was flashing gaily off the white towers of St. James Town and the colourful little cottages of Old Cabbagetown. Neither Boruvka nor I spoke. I was incapable of speech anyway; just keeping the car on course took all the strength and concentration I had. If I didn't believe in guardian angels before, I do now.

I don't know what was going on in the detective's mind. During that daredevil ride, I finally realized how little I understood, not just of the principles of detection (and how dangerous was ignorance in that field!) but of these people who had suddenly brought their bizarre fates into our lives. The owner of *Toronto Lady* and her absurd newspaper; Sue McLaughlin and her Vietnam hero, of whom she refused to be ashamed; the former detective and kidnapper, apparently some kind of martyr, and now practically a member of the *lumpenproletariat*; the singer who had manoeuvred his escape and was now in jail in his place; those parents who had abandoned their child and fled their own country, only to send a gangster with the bizarre alias of Joe Bomb back to reunite the family. What kind of people were they?

I recognized their private emotions, or thought I did, but there seemed to be a legendary dimension to what they did and said. They reminded me of Davy Crockett or Pecos Bill. Then an old memory flashed through my mind. We were on vacation, Heather and I and the parents. She was about eight and I was sixteen, and we were standing on Signal Hill overlooking St. John's, Newfoundland. Dad pointed to the Narrows, where the convoys had entered the harbour during the Second World War, and then said that we were about as close to Europe as we could get without leaving Canada. "What's Europe?" my sister asked.

God knows how we made it. We screamed into Sackville Street and there was Jirina McCavish's white corner house. In front of it was a small flowerbed with coloured blooms and three golden sunflowers towering over it, radiating a brilliant yellow. The little street was quiet and empty. I stopped the motor and listened to the humming of the air conditioners. From the house next door a young girl emerged in shorts and a T-shirt with LOVE, LOVE ME DO on it. She walked towards us. We jumped out of the car.

Precisely at that moment the door of Jirina's house flew open and Herman came rushing out. He crashed into the girl with the inviting T-shirt, knocking her into a flowerbed, then leapt into a car that was parked with two wheels on the sidewalk. Before we could reach him he managed to start the engine and, with a screeching of tires, shot off around the corner into a side street. I ran after him. I knew it was a dead-end street.

But he was only turning around. He stopped the car, threw it into reverse, and backed up as fast as he could. I tried to jump out of the way, and at the same time I instinctively held out my hand to fend off the inevitable impact, but the car caught me and threw me against the townhouse on the corner. My head hit the wall and I sank to the ground. My vision went dark, and in that darkness I heard the grinding of a gearbox as Herman shifted into forward and roared off. With a great effort of will, I opened my eyes just in time to see the car heading south and swerving onto Wellesley.

Slowly I gathered myself up from the ground. The windows of Jirina's house ballooned out and then sank back into their frames. I felt a sharp needle of pain in my hand, and when I took the first step my torn pant-leg flapped open to reveal a bloody knee.

I looked around. The girl in the T-shirt was just climbing out of Jirina's flowerbed. Boruvka was nowhere to be seen. Then I noticed that the door to Jirina's house was ajar, and I held my head for a moment. The world gradually stopped spinning. The girl in the T-shirt was standing in front of me.

"Hey!" she said eagerly. "Are you guys making a movie? Are you a stuntman?"

I walked unsteadily into Jirina's house. The sun was shining through the window onto a white rug where the former detective was kneeling and holding the owner of *Toronto Lady* by the hand. The big, white-faced tomcat was poking his nose into her other hand as it lay limply on the floor; then he began to lick it.

She wasn't dead.

She was, however, unconscious. Blood was soaking from her breast into her white summer dress. Boruvka was holding a short leather strap, and I realized he had just removed it from her hand—it was the strap of her handbag. Someone had tried to tear it from her grasp and, except for the strap, had succeeded.

I looked around. There was no sign of Harrison Morrison.

Boruvka pulled a carefully folded red handkerchief from his pocket and, with a sharp wave of his hand, snapped it open. A red shadow fell across the editor's pale face. The detective stuffed the handkerchief into the bloody wound on her breast.

"Hey!" someone behind us yelled. "Where's the cameras?"

Then a pair of tennis shoes padded rapidly across the rug and a voice said, "My gosh! It's not a movie at all!"

More rapid steps, then a telephone was dialled and a girl's voice said, "Emergency? Send an ambulance to 487 Sackville Street at once, quickly. Someone's been shot!"

I cradled Jirina McCavish's head in my hands. Mr. Boruvka said we weren't to move her until the ambulance came. She was breathing with great difficulty, but there was no blood on her lips. Only that terrible, growing patch of red on her dress—the colour of revolution.

Mr. Boruvka wiped the perspiration from her forehead with his hand and asked the girl in the T-shirt to call the police as well. She did this just as promptly as she'd called the ambulance, then went into the kitchen and came back with a dish-towel soaked in water. Boruvka looked at her gratefully and put the towel on Jirina's forehead. The sadness in his eyes was more painful than my hand, than my head, still reeling from the rye—perhaps even more than the death of my poor sister.

It was a European kind of sadness. Oh God, I thought, I'm not a hard-boiled detective and not even a gallon of Marlowe's whisky in my drawer would make me one. What's going on in this city? My sister, this pretty woman lying here with the red rose of revolution on her breast, the girl with the T-shirt looking for love, the Vietnam warrior's wife with the sad, sad eyes.

Someone was standing in the front doorway, casting a shadow across the rug. I turned around and looked up. A black silhouette stood against the sun, and in one hand I could see the outline of a glistening Colt .45. Then the shadow bolted forward.

Harrison Morrison!

I jumped up and surprised myself with the power that remained in my injured right hand. Harrison went down. The shiny Colt fell to the carpet with a weak thud.

Two other silhouettes appeared in the doorway, wearing policemen's caps. I was almost fainting from the pain shooting up my right arm. An ambulance siren wailed closer and abruptly died.

Then I lost consciousness.

17

A Happy Ending

The detective's daughter had told me once that in her country her father's profession no longer made any sense. And my sister had once asked my father what Europe was.

Perhaps I understand a little better now. After what I went through with these people on the trail of my sister's killer, something of their spirit has got under my skin. They come from a land where politics often seems like a bad soap opera, an endless season of reruns that no one wants to watch, and no one dares ignore. Their history is full of backlashes, and if we long for a history we think we don't possess, they seem to be fugitives from a past that will not be laid to rest.

Yes, Vogeltanz was Bignose, with a nose altered by plastic surgery. The operation had been performed not by some cheap sawbones in a back-street clinic, but by a professor at the Communist Party sanatorium in Prague.

Vogeltanz was one of the means that was justified by the end.

So was Trcka, except that he wasn't a man of Vogeltanz's calibre. He was just a pawn. It's true that in that anomalous year of 1968 (and it was an anomaly everywhere, even here) Interpol were tipped off about him by some liberal security policemen in Prague's newly reformed Ministry of the Interior. But Trcka soon disappeared from sight, around the time when the Russian tanks erased the anomaly.

Both Vogeltanz the Nazi and Trcka the wife-killer were given a choice. A piece of rope or—

In such a situation it must be hard to refuse.

Vogeltanz proved to be worth their while. His SS training turned out to be his most valuable postwar asset. He was suave, worked well under extreme pressure, and could pass for German or Austrian if need be. Sometime in the early 1960s, when the East-West thaw was fast becoming a full-blown spring, he was sent to Toronto, where he established a credible front as the owner of a small international trading company. He wasted no time in developing a sophisticated network of agents who gathered information which he would then personally courier back to his bosses under cover of his business trips.

Ironically, it was Jirina who shattered all those years of quiet Canadian security. Before he met her, Vogeltanz had no idea there was anyone alive who was interested in his former identity, let alone his present job. Then she told him the story of her father's death and her mother's presence of mind during what, for Vogeltanz, had been a routine arrest. Suddenly, the peace of mind he had enjoyed was gone for ever.

He even saw the card with his fingerprints on it—Jirina showed it to him. So he had the idea of staging a mugging to cover up the switch, probably with Trcka's help. It was easy to make a card with false prints; cards encased in plastic didn't differ much. Only when he had the incriminating card did he realize it wasn't the original—why else would Jirina have written *copy* on the back? So he decided on a revolutionary solution. But like all great revolutionaries, he didn't have to do his dirty work himself. His recently acquired agent was a common murderer who had killed his ex-wife because he couldn't get her out of the house. The Party has ways of getting embarrassments like Trcka safely out of its hair, but it exacts a high price for such salvation. Trcka had to do precisely what he was told, or Interpol would receive an anonymous tip and that would be the end of him. When Vogeltanz's bosses had found Trcka in a refugee camp in Italy they had given him new identity papers, but nobody could give him new fingerprints.

Vogeltanz's bosses got Trcka into Canada, where he was run by Vogeltanz. But when Vogeltanz gave him his one big assignment, Trcka botched it. Trcka didn't know Jirina. And so Heather died in her place. Trcka had already been trying his bosses' patience with his hare-brained schemes to defraud the gullible, and he knew that a failure of this magnitude would mean the end of his career in Canada, if not the end altogether. He lost his nerve, and put an end to his problems.

Or maybe they got to him first.

However it was, Trcka's immediate superior, Vogeltanz, now had to act for himself and eventually he became hopelessly entangled in the whole mess. He even nearly eliminated an innocent observer, Nikola Krsic, who served him only as a means of exit from his own particular locked room. Fortunately the tough, fornicating partisan survived, though the blow on the head seems to have done something to his libido. But Vogeltanz's career, such as it was, was a shambles.

Had he managed to wipe out that last shred of evidence from the past, from that single careless rifling through a single well-stocked bookshelf, then perhaps he might have been given a new identity, new papers, and a new mission. After all, he was no ordinary informer. The reports he passed on to his superiors had nothing to do with the love lives and petty rivalries of a rather insignificant ethnic community in Toronto, although no doubt the casual conversations overheard at the Old English Pub provided him with amusing material for his superiors in lean periods.

As it was, Vogeltanz vanished. The RCMP were alerted at once, of course, but they were never able to run him to ground on Canadian territory, even though they admitted to me privately that they had been aware of Vogeltanz's existence. Who knows? Boruvka says agents working at Vogeltanz's level always have back doors close at hand. But Interpol had his dossier as well, and unless he managed to get in out of the cold, back to the Soviet bloc, his life can't be pleasant. Even there, Boruvka says, he would be far from secure. Agents who have outlived their usefulness quickly learn that the art of survival means the art of avoiding car accidents, mushroom poisoning, sudden strokes, or mysterious occurrences of malignant tumours.

It's Boruvka's feeling that Vogeltanz will not be one of the lucky survivors. If he's right, that's the final irony—that the agent of justice will be the system that, in a sense, was responsible for the crime in the first place.

Sheila and I took our four-year-old daughter, Heather, to the wedding in Memphis, Tennessee. It was a traditional wedding in a Catholic church, with the bride in white, though at her age—but these days, such things are irrelevant. Heather carried the bride's train, which was so heavy she stumbled and fell on the way to the altar and scraped her nose.

How the bride got from Prague to Memphis is a saga best left for another time. I still find it hard to believe some of the details myself. But it was quite touching to see the mournful detective looking so happy.

There was a second bridesmaid, a fifteen-year-old girl from Pittsburgh. She came with her parents, who thanked the former detective with tears in their eyes, though they weren't related to the bride at all. They also seemed very attached to a fellow in an American Airlines uniform who stopped by on his way to the airport.

The wedding supper took place at Sue McLaughlin's house. Her husband, the Vietnam vet, has finished his studies and is now teaching in Memphis. Mack got pleasantly smashed in a well-decorated dress uniform of a U.S. Army officer. It seemed a little out of place.

Jirina Chumac, who otherwise had no special responsibilities, made sure that everyone was properly entertained.

Herman himself didn't come. He said he was too busy but I think there were other reasons. He's still ashamed at how he panicked back then and went for the ambulance by car instead of using the telephone, almost killing me while he was at it.

On the other hand, Harrison Morrison was brave enough to show up, and he brought along a barrel of a new beer called Megan's Brew that left me with a terrible headache the next day. Fool. When I'd hung up that time, he'd suddenly lost faith in karate and gone to buy bullets for the Colt. Since then, I've had at least one weapon to use against him if it ever occurred to him to become sarcastic about how Sheila and I almost blew the case.

Except for the obligatory toast, Sheila didn't drink at the wedding—not even Harrison's newest Limbo Springs concoction. Before we decided to have Heather, she realized—with some help from me—that her emulation of Philip Marlowe, if not detrimental to her own health, could have adverse effects on our offspring. She took the cure, and it was unusually successful. Maybe the old-fashioned feminine joy of having a baby contributed to the success.

And that's all.

A happy ending.

I do believe that. I'm North American. Here happy endings are still possible, although in Europe, it seems, they no longer exist. Certainly not in that *other* Europe, as Boruvka might say.

All the same, I seem to have caught at least something of that oppressive disease, the European virus. A melancholy that sometimes knocks me off my feet and eats away at the very substance of my optimism. Perhaps I'll recover. It depends.

While Sheila (who no longer has her Watchful Sisters) and I said goodbye to Boruvka and his bride, Eve, at a corner bar in Memphis, I told him about it. I said we both understood him better now. Sheila and I had realized, each in our own way, that when you breathe, you have to have air. It's a wonderful thing to be able to take the air for granted, but in this world that's no longer possible.

Yet as long as we're breathing, there's hope. Everything, finally, will turn out right. I still believe that.

"I believe so too," said Mr. Boruvka. "Not to hope would be against human nature." He looked at me with his forget-me-not eyes, and despite his momentary personal happiness they were still full of that ineradicable sadness. His round face glowed pink against the background of multi-coloured labels and bottles of bourbon and vodka and gin and Scotch and Southern Comfort.

"Then why do you always look so sad?" asked Sheila.

Mr. Boruvka took a gloomy sip and looked at us with his baleful eyes. "*Spes longa*—not that I remember much Latin, just a few fragments from high school," he said awkwardly. "But you know—*vita brevis. Brevis....*"

What he meant by that I couldn't say, for although I took Latin in high school too, I never finished the course.

JOSEF SKVORECKY is Professor of English at Erindale College, University of Toronto. He emigrated to Canada after the Soviet invasion of Czechoslovakia in 1968, and he and his wife, the novelist Zdena Salivarova, continue to keep Czech literature alive through their Czech-language publishing house, 68 Publishers. Skvorecky was the 1980 winner of the Neustadt International Prize for Literature and was nominated in 1982 for the Nobel Prize. His fiction includes *The Cowards*, *Miss Silver's Past*, *The Bass Saxophone*, *The Swell Season*, *The Engineer of Human Souls* (winner of the 1984 Governor General's Award), *Dvorak in Love*, and the Boruvka detective series (*The Mournful Demeanour of Lieutenant Boruvka*, *Sins for Father Knox*, *The End of Lieutenant Boruvka*, and *The Return of Lieutenant Boruvka*). His essays are collected in *Talkin' Moscow Blues*, edited by Sam Solecki.

PAUL WILSON lived in Czechoslovakia for ten years, working as a translator and English teacher, and playing with an underground rock band, The Plastic People of the Universe. He was expelled in 1977. In addition to other novels and stories by Josef Skvorecky, he has translated works by many Czech authors, including Vaclav Havel and Bohumil Hrabal. He now lives in Toronto.